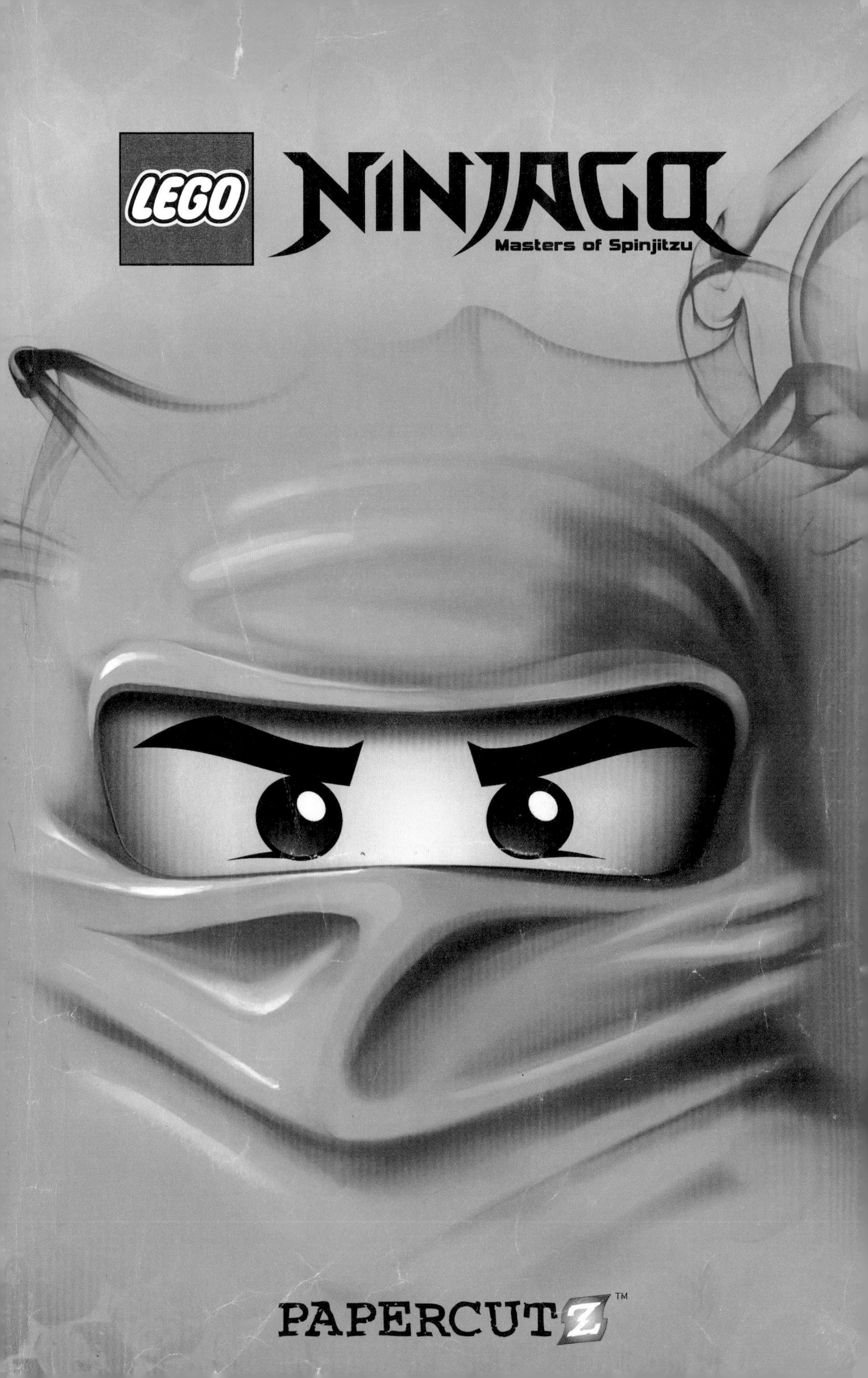
LEGO
NINJAGO
Masters of Spinjitzu
PAPERCUTZ

LEGO® GRAPHIC NOVELS AVAILABLE FROM PAPERCUTZ™

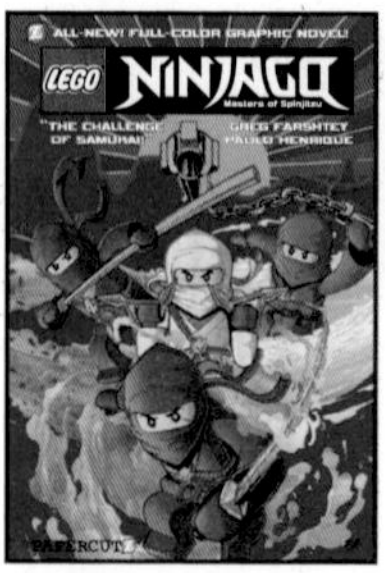
NINJAGO
"THE CHALLENGE OF SAMUKAI"
LEGO NINJAGO #1

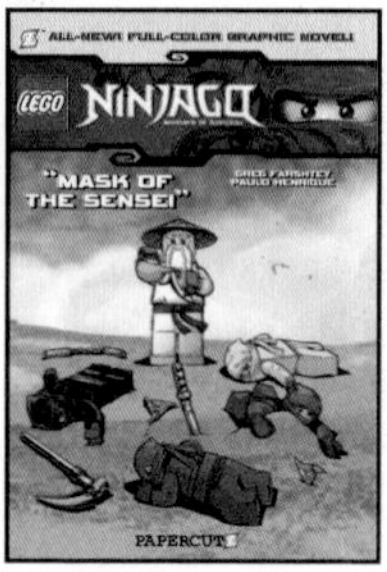
NINJAGO
"MASK OF THE SENSEI"
LEGO NINJAGO #2

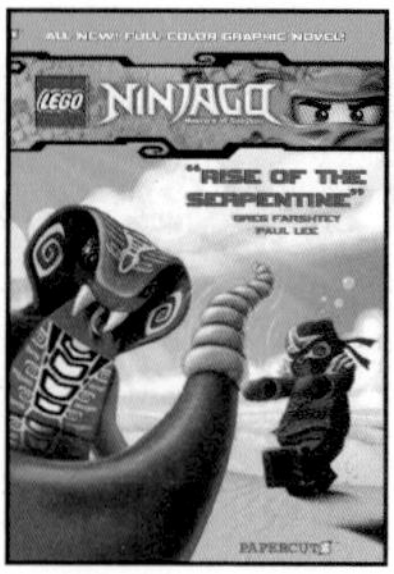
NINJAGO
"RISE OF THE SERPENTINE"
LEGO NINJAGO #3

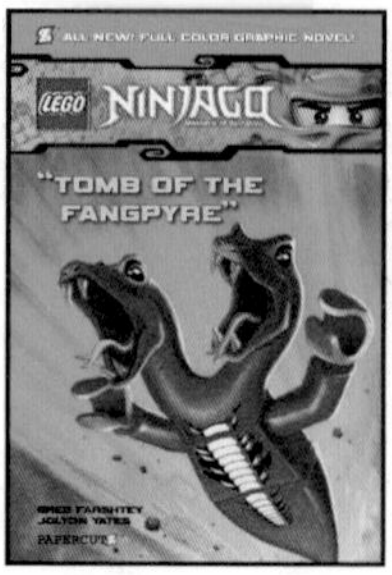
NINJAGO
"TOMB OF THE FANGPYRE"
LEGO NINJAGO #4

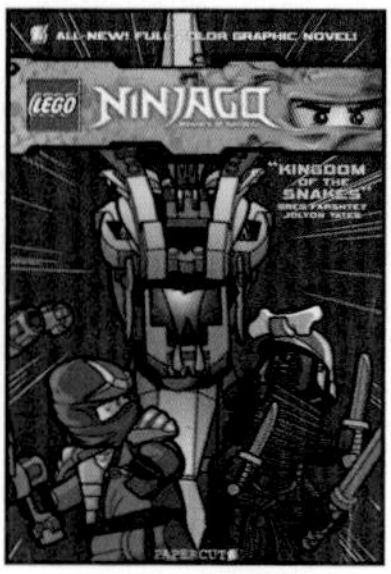
NINJAGO
"KINGDOM OF THE SNAKES"
LEGO NINJAGO #5

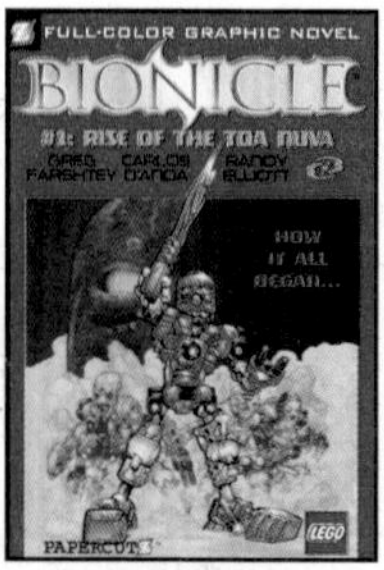
FULL-COLOR GRAPHIC NOVEL
BIONICLE
#1: RISE OF THE TOA NUVA
BIONICLE #1

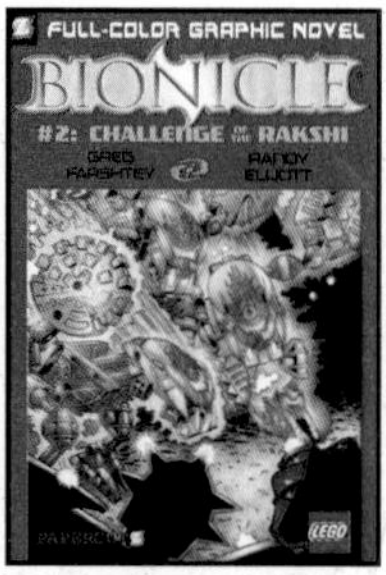
FULL-COLOR GRAPHIC NOVEL
BIONICLE
#2: CHALLENGE OF THE RAKSHI
BIONICLE #2

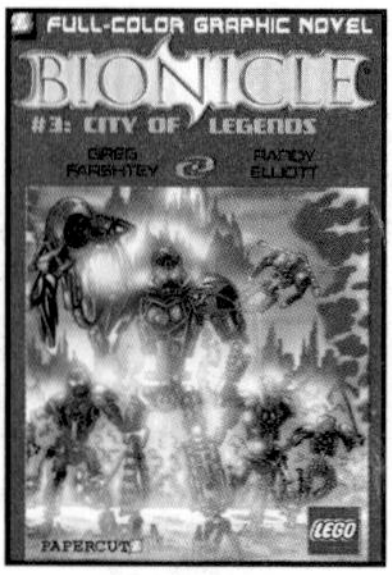
FULL-COLOR GRAPHIC NOVEL
BIONICLE
#3: CITY OF LEGENDS
BIONICLE #3

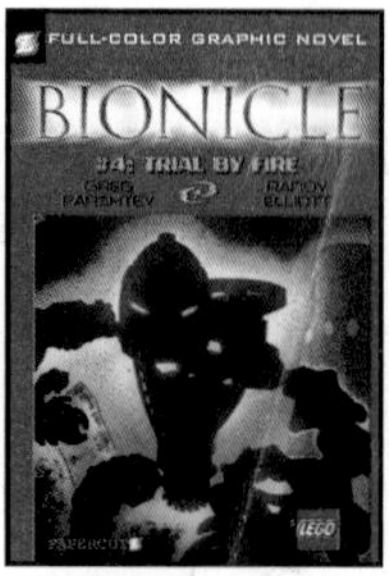
FULL-COLOR GRAPHIC NOVEL
BIONICLE
#4: TRIAL BY FIRE
BIONICLE #4

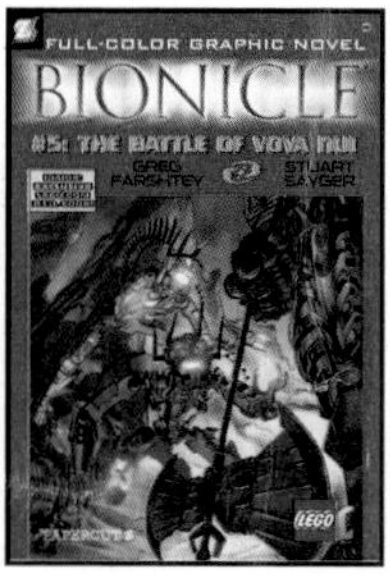
FULL-COLOR GRAPHIC NOVEL
BIONICLE
#5: THE BATTLE OF VOYA NUI
BIONICLE #5

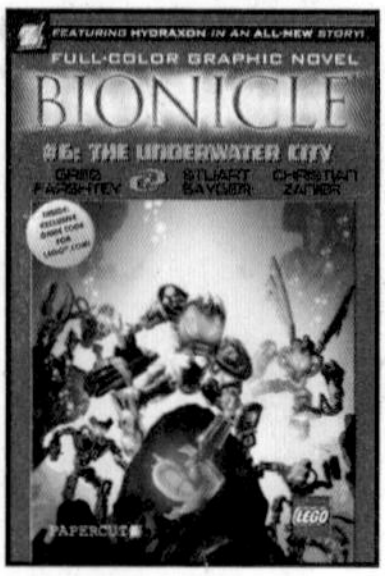
FULL-COLOR GRAPHIC NOVEL
BIONICLE
#6: THE UNDERWATER CITY
BIONICLE #6

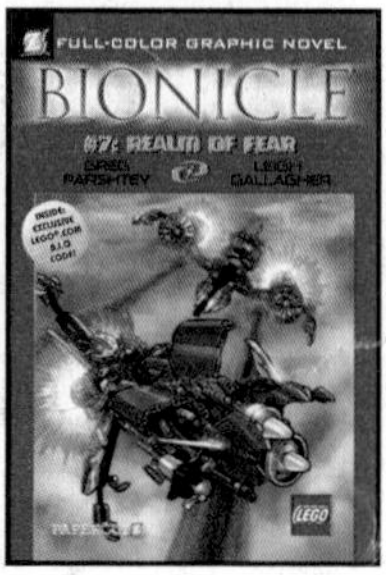
FULL-COLOR GRAPHIC NOVEL
BIONICLE
#7: REALM OF FEAR
BIONICLE #7

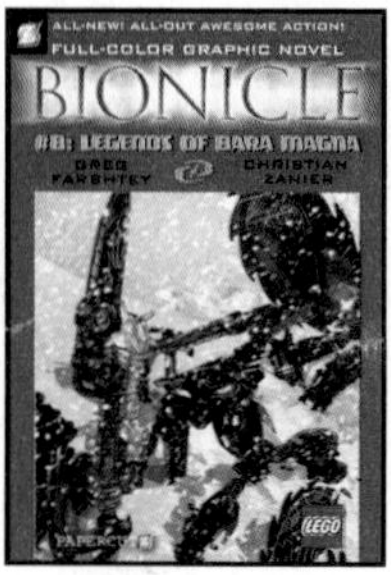
FULL-COLOR GRAPHIC NOVEL
BIONICLE
#8: LEGENDS OF BARA MAGNA
BIONICLE #8

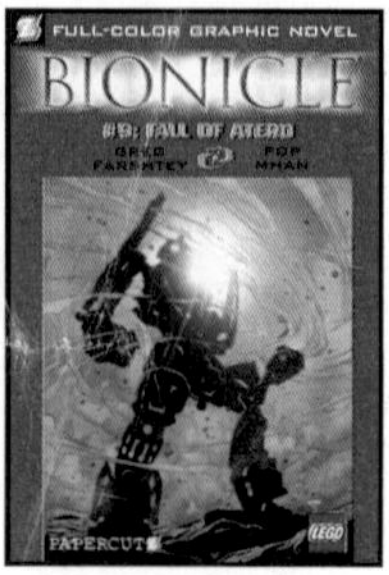
FULL-COLOR GRAPHIC NOVEL
BIONICLE
#9: FALL OF ATERO
BIONICLE #9

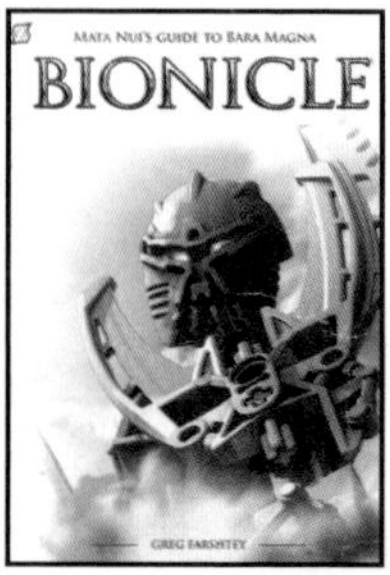
MATA NUI'S GUIDE TO BARA MAGNA
BIONICLE
Mata Nui's Guide to Bara Magna

LEGO NINJAGO graphic novels, BIONICLE® graphic novels, and guide books are available in paperback and hardcover at booksellers everywhere.

Or order from us: please add $4.00 for postage and handling for first book, add $1.00 for each additional book.
LEGO NINJAGO #1-5 are $6.99 in paperback, and $13.99 in hardcover.
BIONICLE #1-3, 8, and 9 are $8.99 in paperback, $13.99 in hardcover.
BIONICLE #4-7 are $7.95 in paperback and $12.95 in hardcover.
Guide Books are $9.99 each in paperback only.
Please make check payable to NBM Publishing.

Send to: Papercutz, 160 Broadway, Suite 700, East Wing, New York, NY 10038

Or call 800-886-1223 between 9-5 EST, M-F. Visa, MC, and AmEx accepted.

www.papercutz.com

LEGO NINJAGO graphic novels are also available digitally wherever e-books are sold.

LEGO NINJAGO
Masters of Spinjitzu

#5 "KINGDOM OF THE SNAKES"

Greg Farshtey – Writer
Jolyon Yates – Artist
Jayjay Jackson – Colorist
Paul Lee – Cover Artist
Laurie E. Smith – Cover Colorist

PAPERCUTZ
New York

LEGO® NINJAGO Masters of Spinjitzu
#5 "Kingdom of the Snakes"

GREG FARSHTEY – Writer
JOLYON YATES – Artist
JAYJAY JACKSON – Colorist
BRYAN SENKA – Letterer
NELSON DESIGN GROUP, LLC – Production
JACK "KING" KIRBY – Special Thanks
BETH SCORZATO – Production Coordinator
MICHAEL PETRANEK – Associate Editor
JIM SALICRUP
Editor-in-Chief

ISBN: 978-1-59707-356-1 paperback edition
ISBN: 978-1-59707-357-8 hardcover edition

Printed in the USA
May 2013 by Bang Printing
3323 Oak Street
Brainerd, MN 56401

Papercutz books may be purchased for business or promotional use. For information on bulk purchases please contact Macmillan
Corporate and Premium Sales Department at (800) 221-7945 x5442.

Distributed by Macmillan

Third Printing

MEET THE MASTERS OF SPINJITZU...

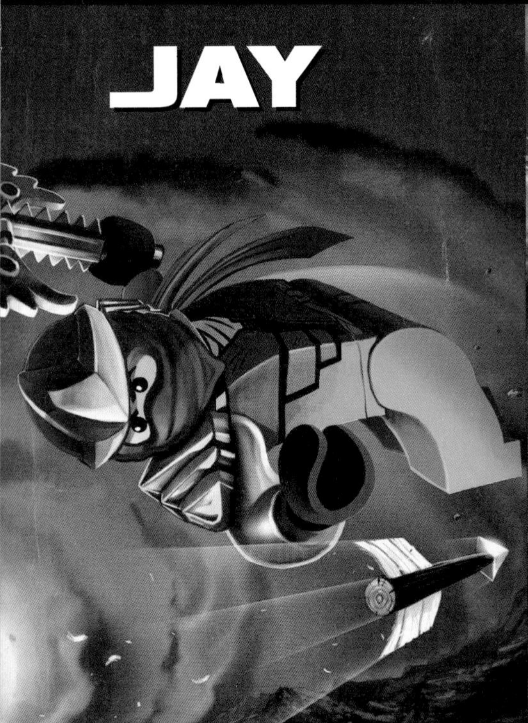
JAY

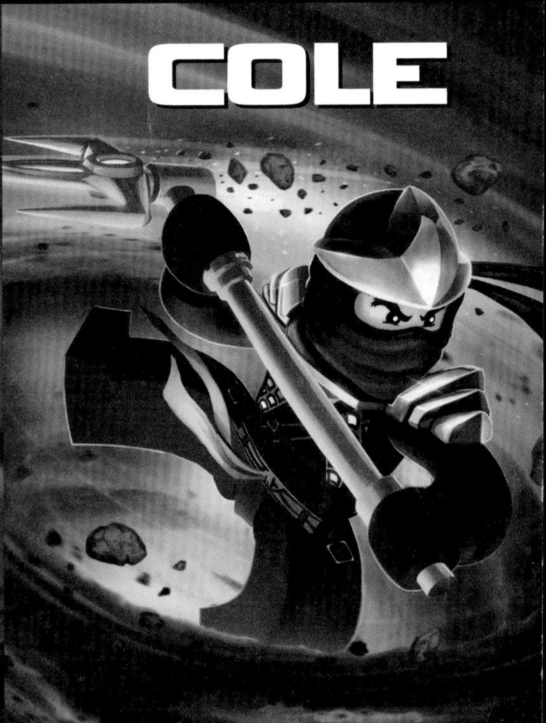
COLE

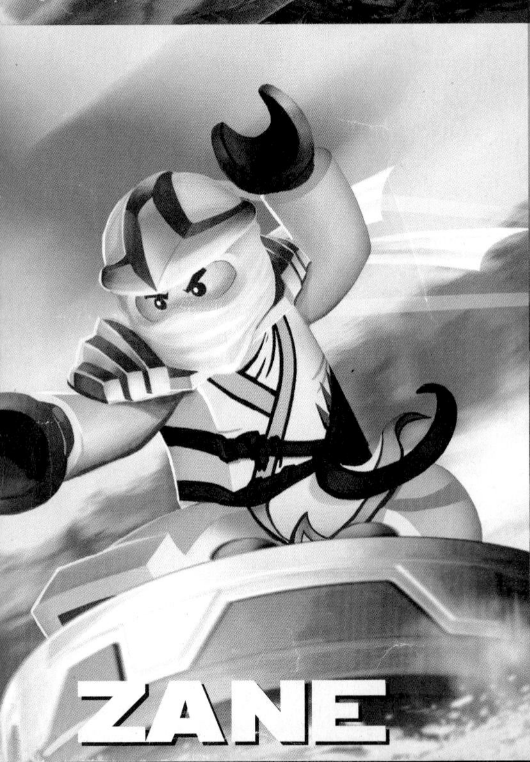
ZANE

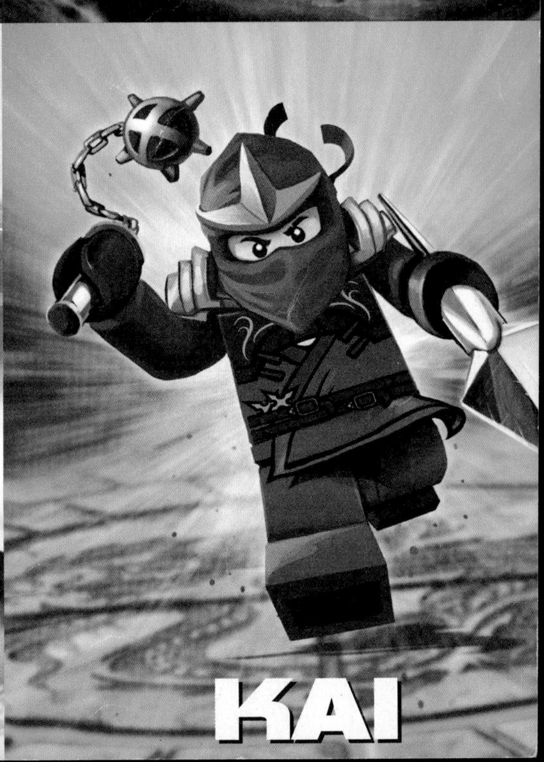
KAI

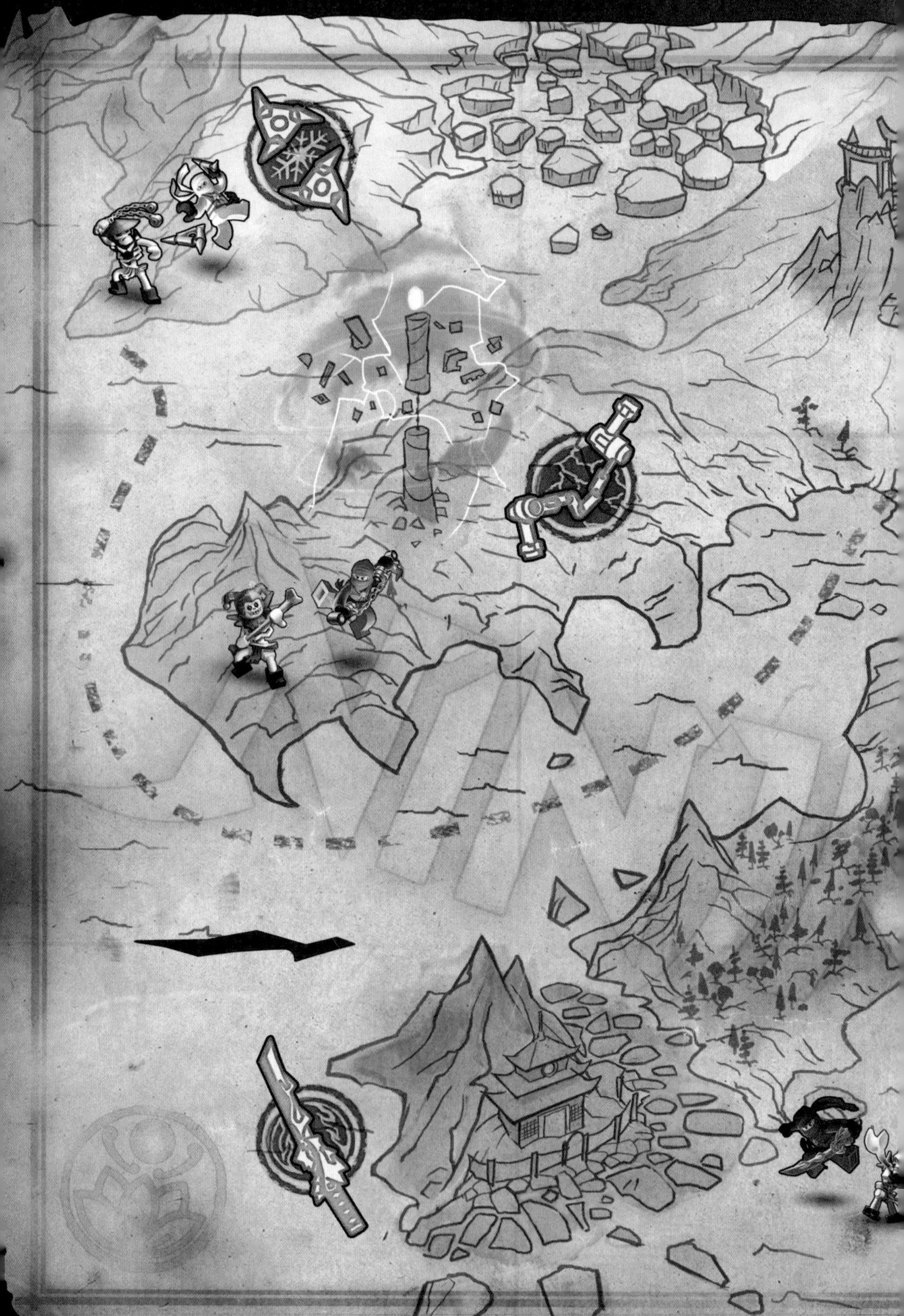

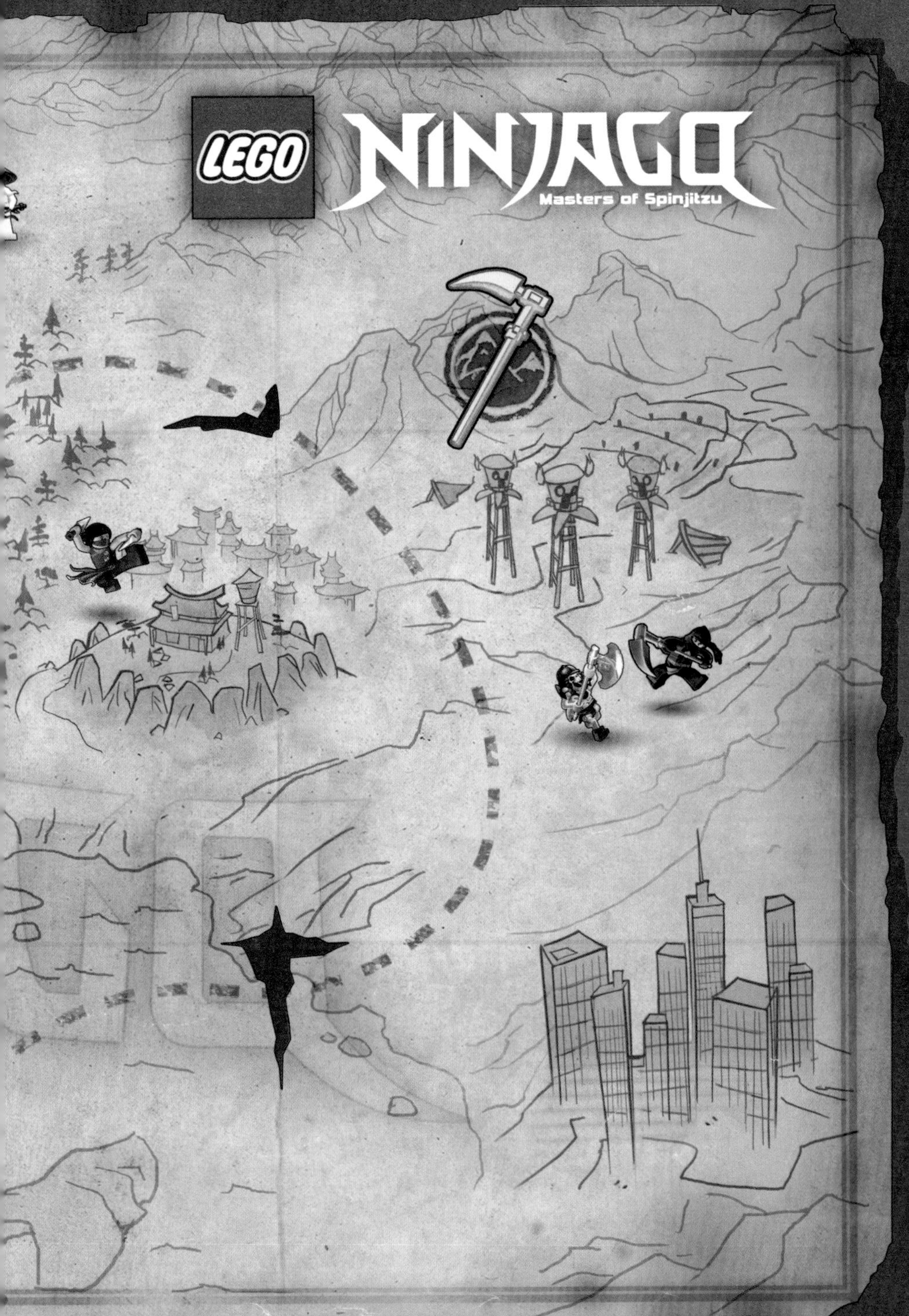

And the Master of the Masters of Spinjitzu...

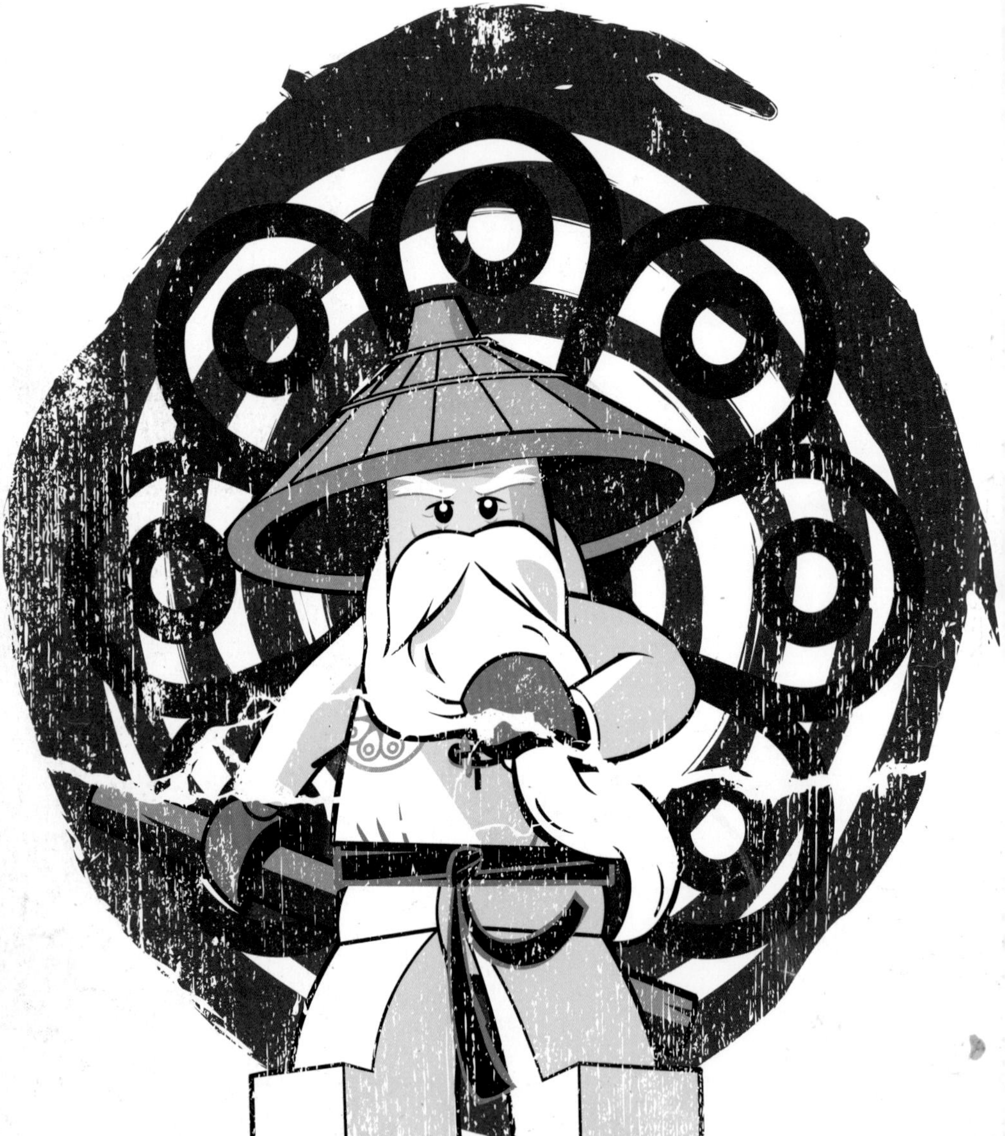

SENSEI WU

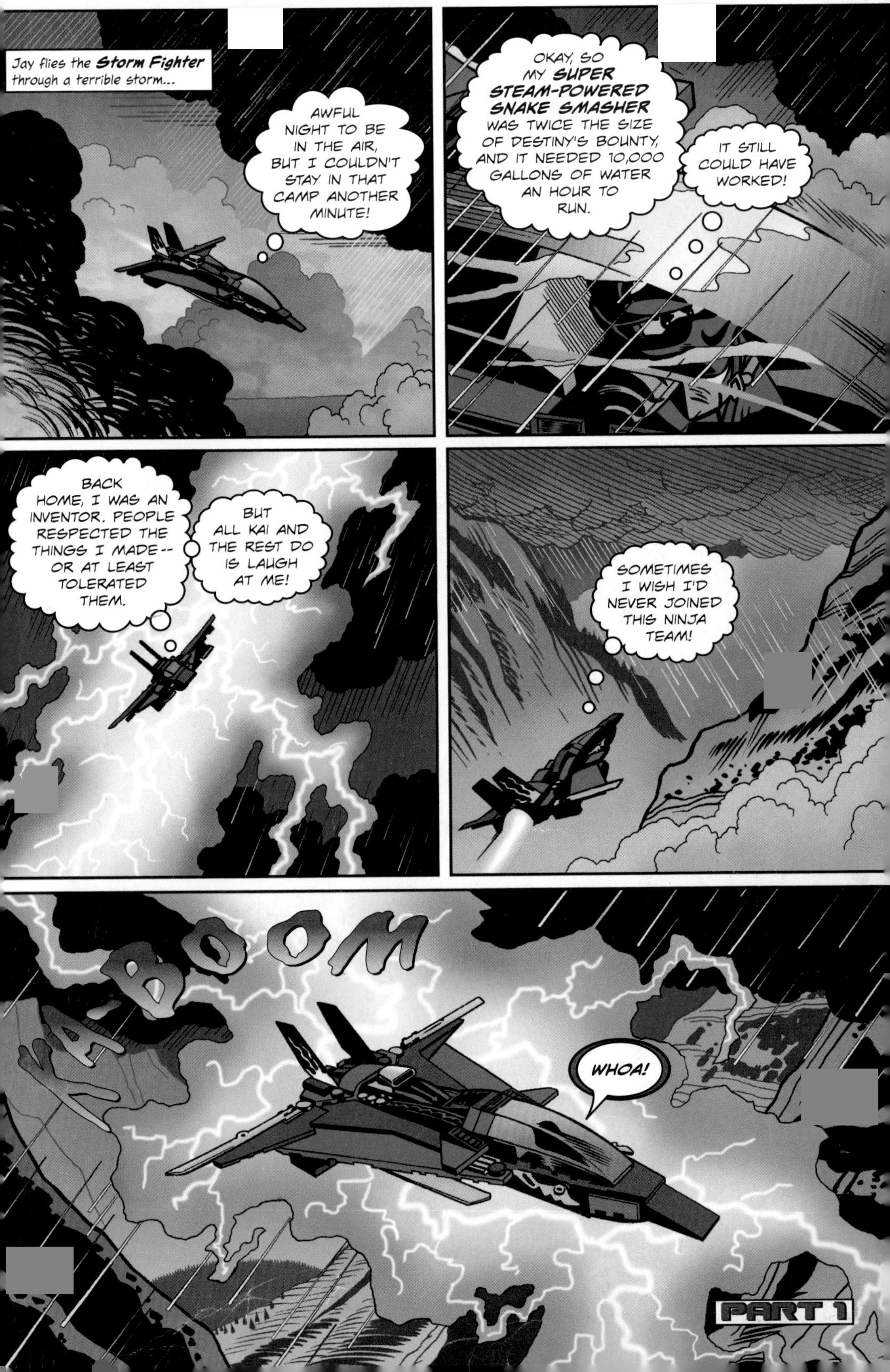
Jay flies the **Storm Fighter** through a terrible storm...
AWFUL NIGHT TO BE IN THE AIR, BUT I COULDN'T STAY IN THAT CAMP ANOTHER MINUTE!
OKAY, SO MY **SUPER STEAM-POWERED SNAKE SMASHER** WAS TWICE THE SIZE OF DESTINY'S BOUNTY, AND IT NEEDED 10,000 GALLONS OF WATER AN HOUR TO RUN.
IT STILL COULD HAVE WORKED!
BACK HOME, I WAS AN INVENTOR. PEOPLE RESPECTED THE THINGS I MADE-- OR AT LEAST TOLERATED THEM.
BUT ALL KAI AND THE REST DO IS LAUGH AT ME!
SOMETIMES I WISH I'D NEVER JOINED THIS NINJA TEAM!
KABOOM
WHOA!
PART 1

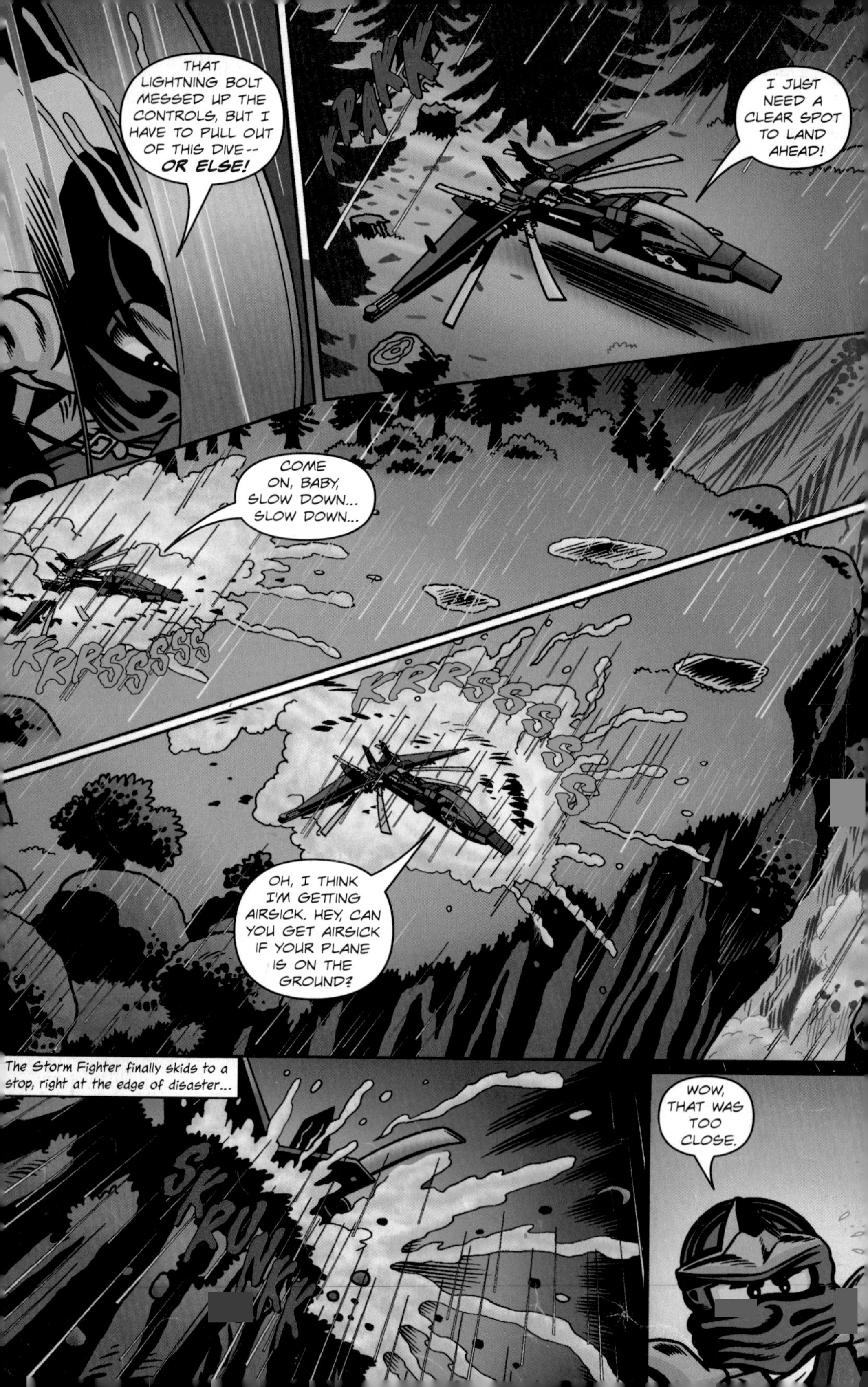
THAT LIGHTNING BOLT MESSED UP THE CONTROLS, BUT I HAVE TO PULL OUT OF THIS DIVE-- **OR ELSE!**
KRAKK
I JUST NEED A CLEAR SPOT TO LAND AHEAD!
COME ON, BABY, SLOW DOWN... SLOW DOWN...
KRRSSSSSS
KRRSSSSSS
OH, I THINK I'M GETTING AIRSICK. HEY, CAN YOU GET AIRSICK IF YOUR PLANE IS ON THE GROUND?
The Storm Fighter finally skids to a stop, right at the edge of disaster...
SKRUNKK
WOW, THAT WAS TOO CLOSE.

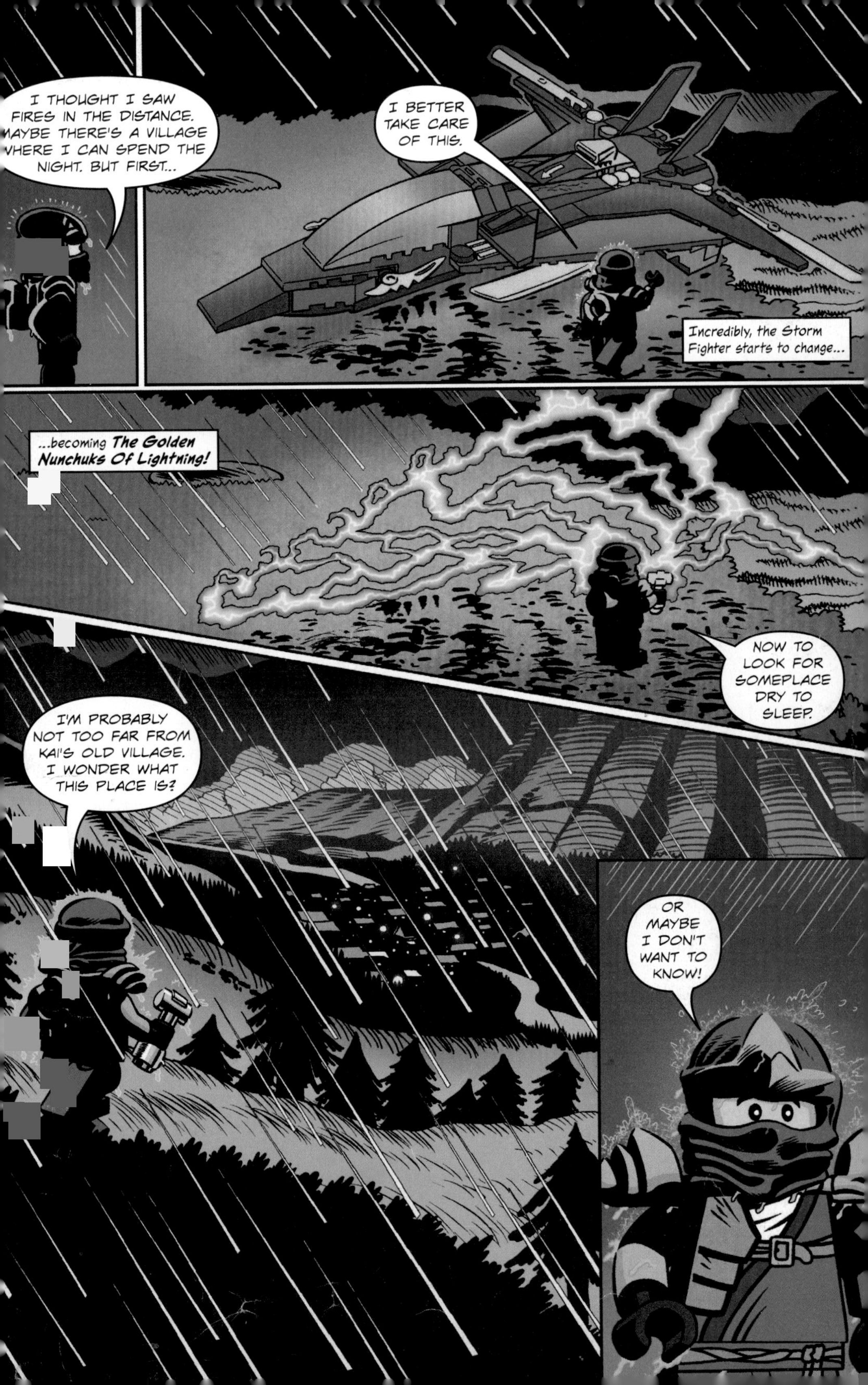
I THOUGHT I SAW FIRES IN THE DISTANCE. MAYBE THERE'S A VILLAGE WHERE I CAN SPEND THE NIGHT. BUT FIRST...
I BETTER TAKE CARE OF THIS.
Incredibly, the Storm Fighter starts to change...
...becoming The Golden Nunchuks Of Lightning!
NOW TO LOOK FOR SOMEPLACE DRY TO SLEEP.
I'M PROBABLY NOT TOO FAR FROM KAI'S OLD VILLAGE. I WONDER WHAT THIS PLACE IS?
OR MAYBE I DON'T WANT TO KNOW!

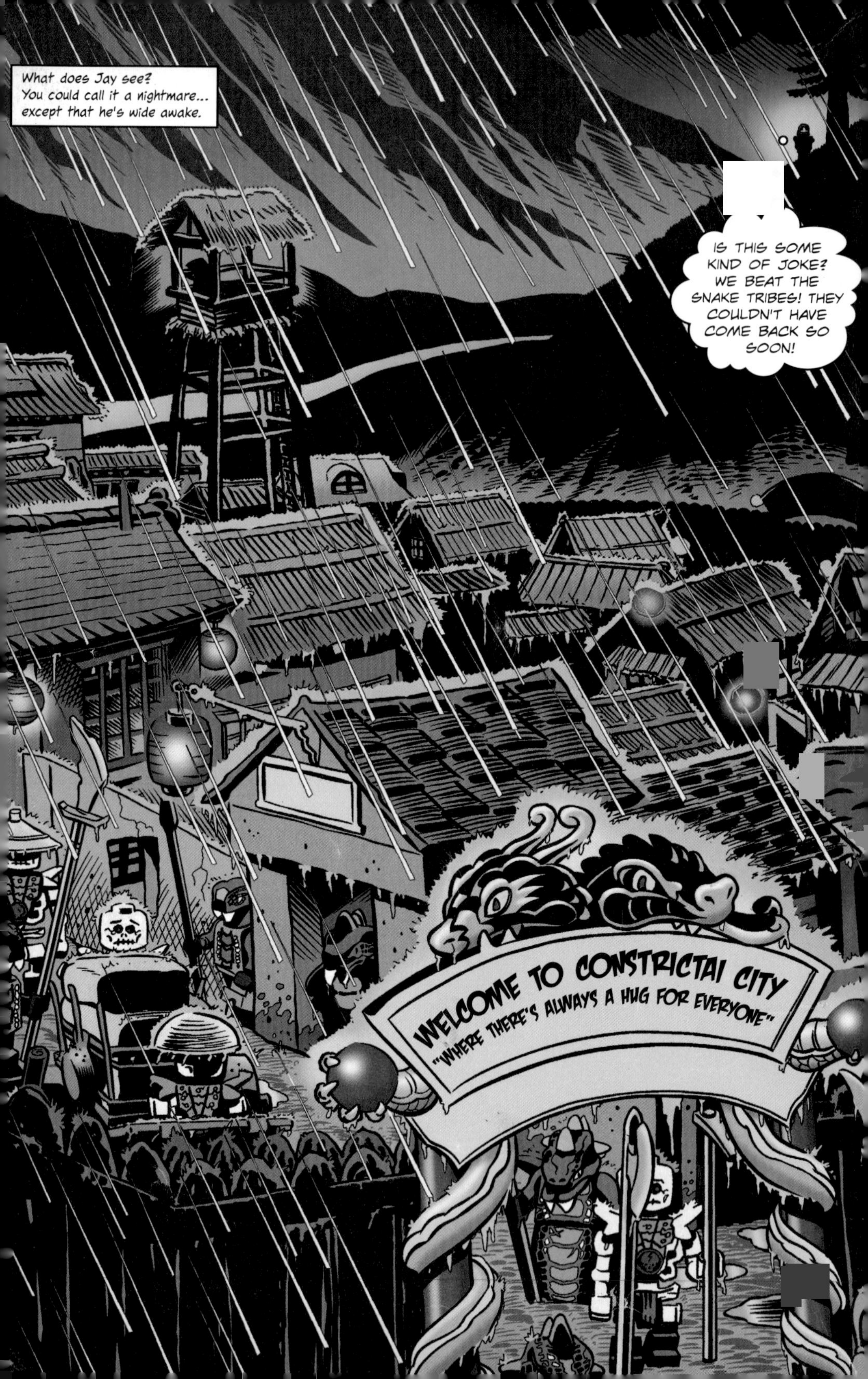
What does Jay see?
You could call it a nightmare...
except that he's wide awake.
IS THIS SOME KIND OF JOKE? WE BEAT THE SNAKE TRIBES! THEY COULDN'T HAVE COME BACK SO SOON!
WELCOME TO CONSTRICTAI CITY
"WHERE THERE'S ALWAYS A HUG FOR EVERYONE"

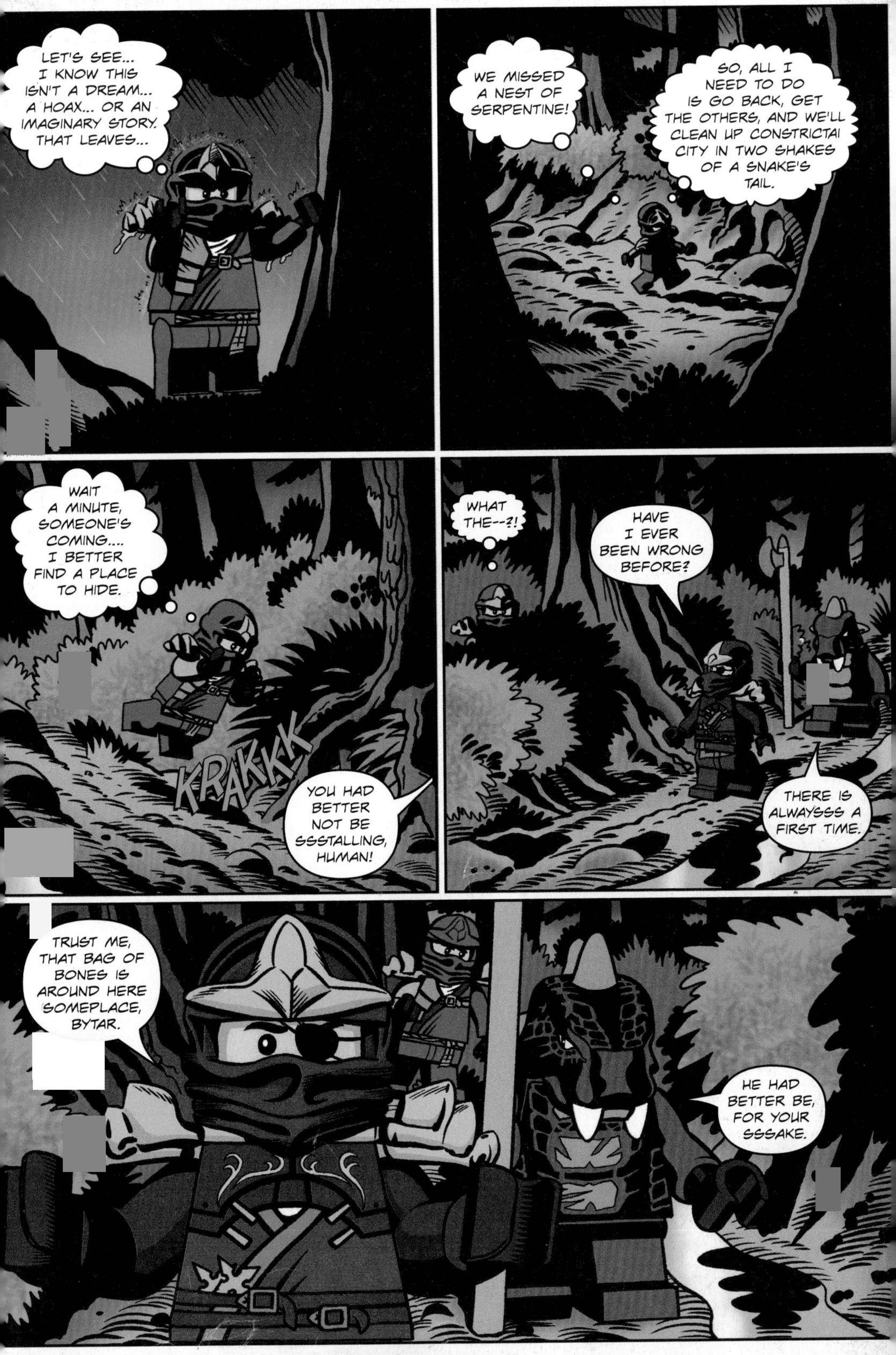
LET'S SEE... I KNOW THIS ISN'T A DREAM... A HOAX... OR AN IMAGINARY STORY. THAT LEAVES...
WE MISSED A NEST OF SERPENTINE!
SO, ALL I NEED TO DO IS GO BACK, GET THE OTHERS, AND WE'LL CLEAN UP CONSTRICTAI CITY IN TWO SHAKES OF A SNAKE'S TAIL.
WAIT A MINUTE, SOMEONE'S COMING.... I BETTER FIND A PLACE TO HIDE.
KRAKKK
YOU HAD BETTER NOT BE SSSTALLING, HUMAN!
WHAT THE--?!
HAVE I EVER BEEN WRONG BEFORE?
THERE IS ALWAYSSS A FIRST TIME.
TRUST ME, THAT BAG OF BONES IS AROUND HERE SOMEPLACE, BYTAR.
HE HAD BETTER BE, FOR YOUR SSSAKE.

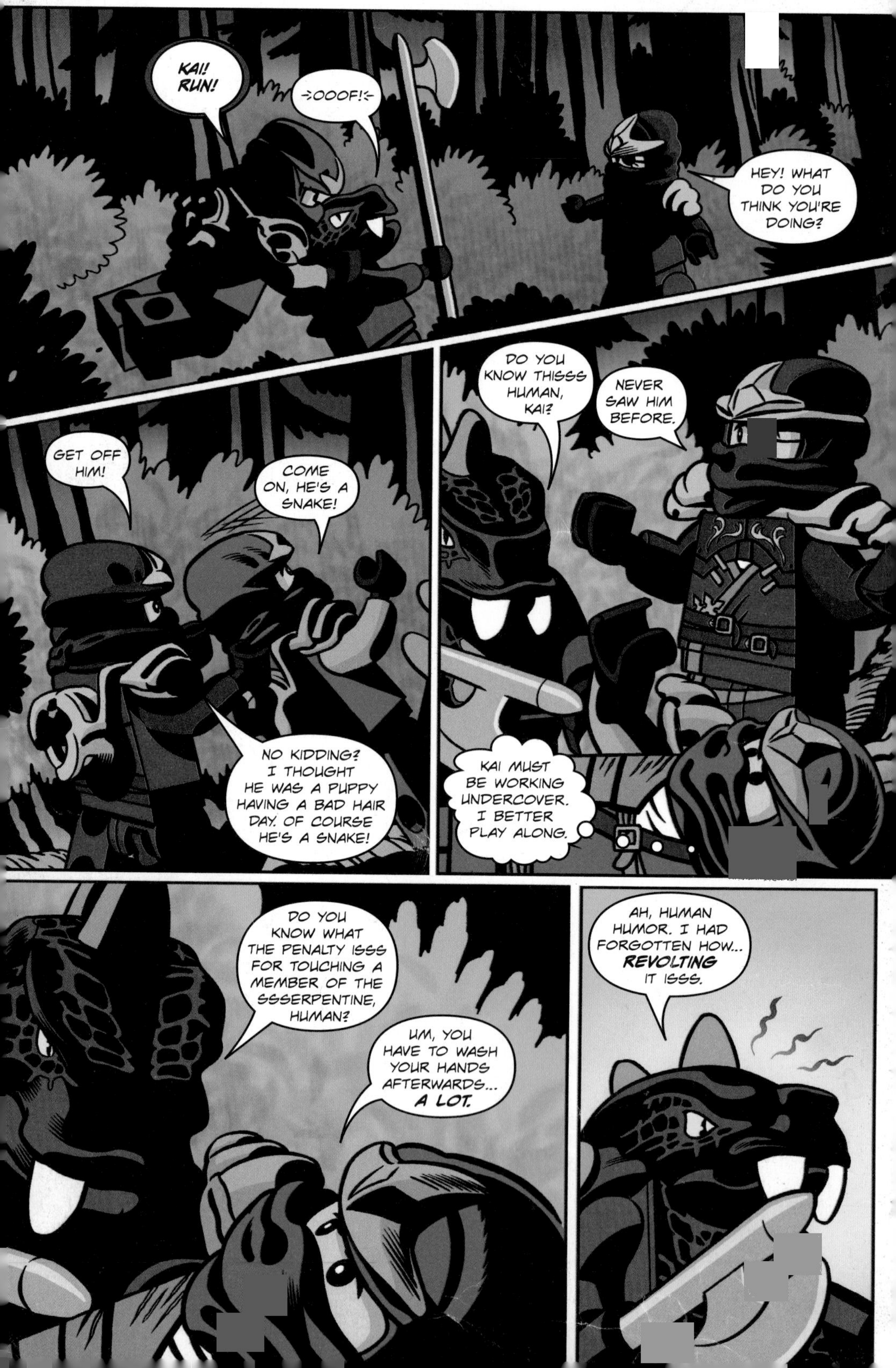
KAI! RUN!
OOOF!
HEY! WHAT DO YOU THINK YOU'RE DOING?
GET OFF HIM!
COME ON, HE'S A SNAKE!
NO KIDDING? I THOUGHT HE WAS A PUPPY HAVING A BAD HAIR DAY. OF COURSE HE'S A SNAKE!
DO YOU KNOW THISSS HUMAN, KAI?
NEVER SAW HIM BEFORE.
KAI MUST BE WORKING UNDERCOVER. I BETTER PLAY ALONG.
DO YOU KNOW WHAT THE PENALTY ISSS FOR TOUCHING A MEMBER OF THE SSSERPENTINE, HUMAN?
UM, YOU HAVE TO WASH YOUR HANDS AFTERWARDS... **A LOT.**
AH, HUMAN HUMOR. I HAD FORGOTTEN HOW... **REVOLTING** IT ISSS.

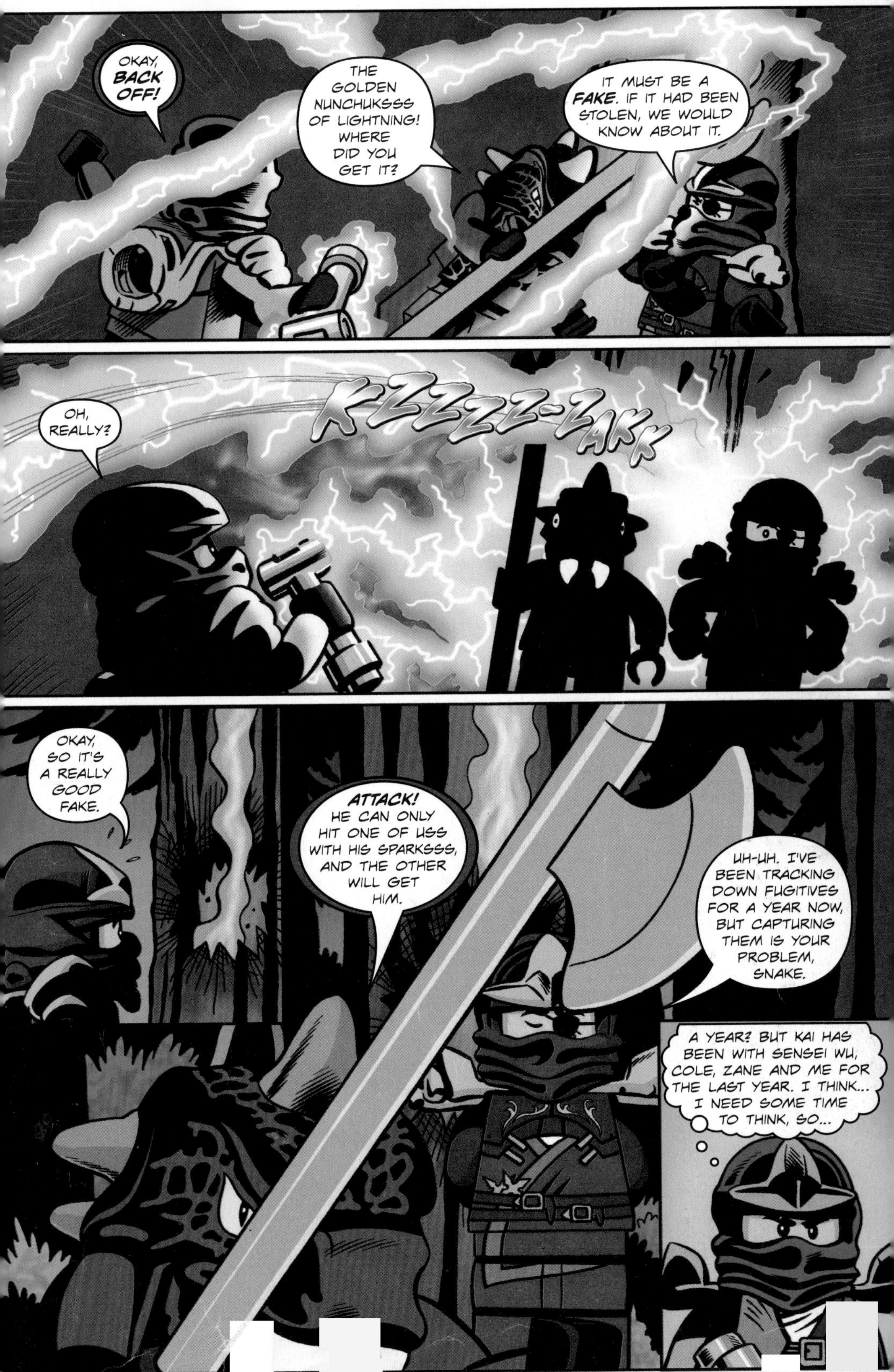
OKAY, BACK OFF!
THE GOLDEN NUNCHUKSSS OF LIGHTNING! WHERE DID YOU GET IT?
IT MUST BE A FAKE. IF IT HAD BEEN STOLEN, WE WOULD KNOW ABOUT IT.
OH, REALLY?
K-ZZZZZ-ZAKK
OKAY, SO IT'S A REALLY GOOD FAKE.
ATTACK! HE CAN ONLY HIT ONE OF USS WITH HIS SPARKSSS, AND THE OTHER WILL GET HIM.
UH-UH. I'VE BEEN TRACKING DOWN FUGITIVES FOR A YEAR NOW, BUT CAPTURING THEM IS YOUR PROBLEM, SNAKE.
A YEAR? BUT KAI HAS BEEN WITH SENSEI WU, COLE, ZANE AND ME FOR THE LAST YEAR. I THINK... I NEED SOME TIME TO THINK, SO...

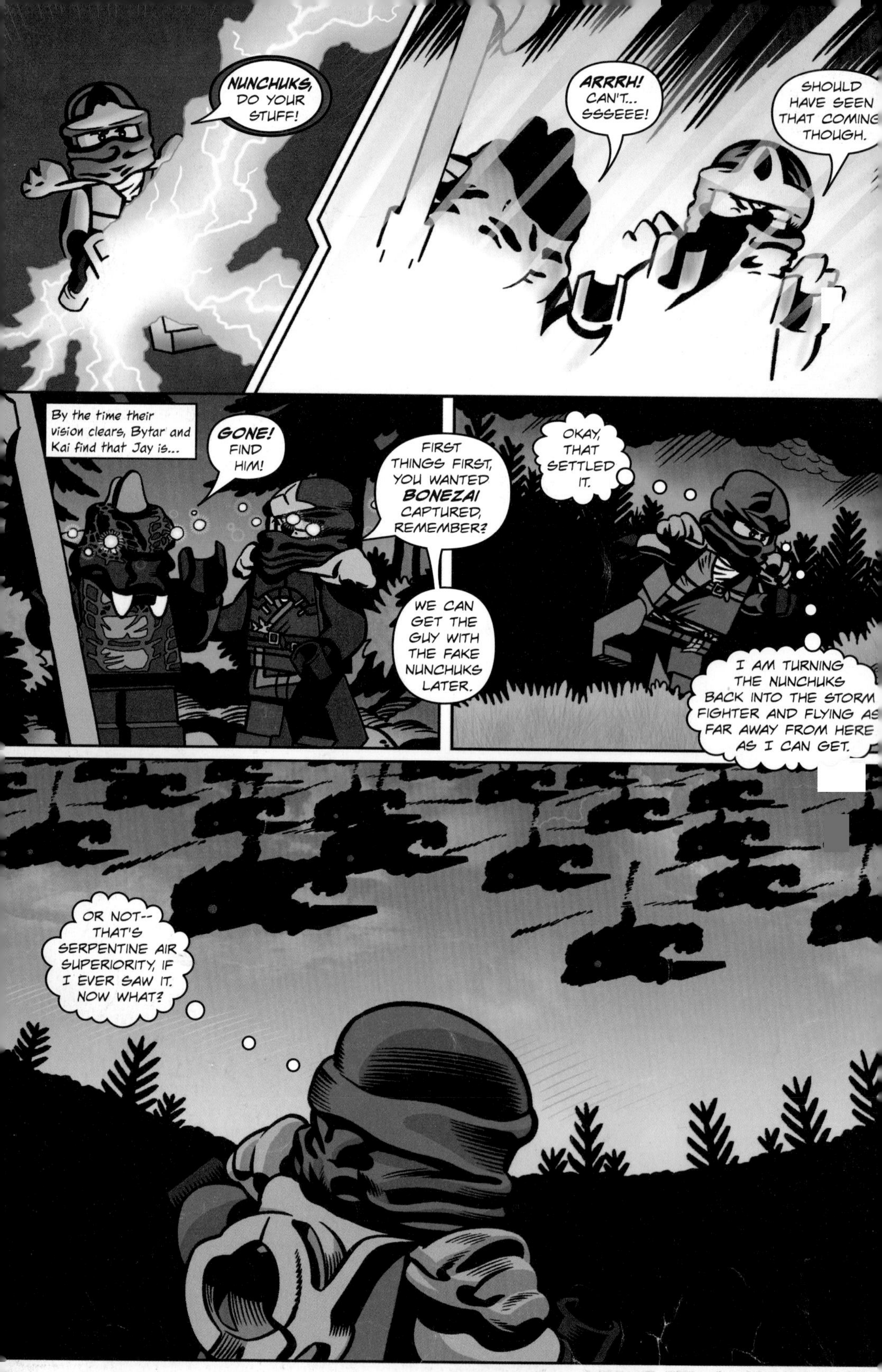
NUNCHUKS, DO YOUR STUFF!
ARRRH! CAN'T... SSSEEE!
SHOULD HAVE SEEN THAT COMING THOUGH.
By the time their vision clears, Bytar and Kai find that Jay is...
GONE! FIND HIM!
FIRST THINGS FIRST, YOU WANTED BONEZAI CAPTURED, REMEMBER?
WE CAN GET THE GUY WITH THE FAKE NUNCHUKS LATER.
OKAY, THAT SETTLED IT.
I AM TURNING THE NUNCHUKS BACK INTO THE STORM FIGHTER AND FLYING AS FAR AWAY FROM HERE AS I CAN GET.
OR NOT-- THAT'S SERPENTINE AIR SUPERIORITY, IF I EVER SAW IT. NOW WHAT?

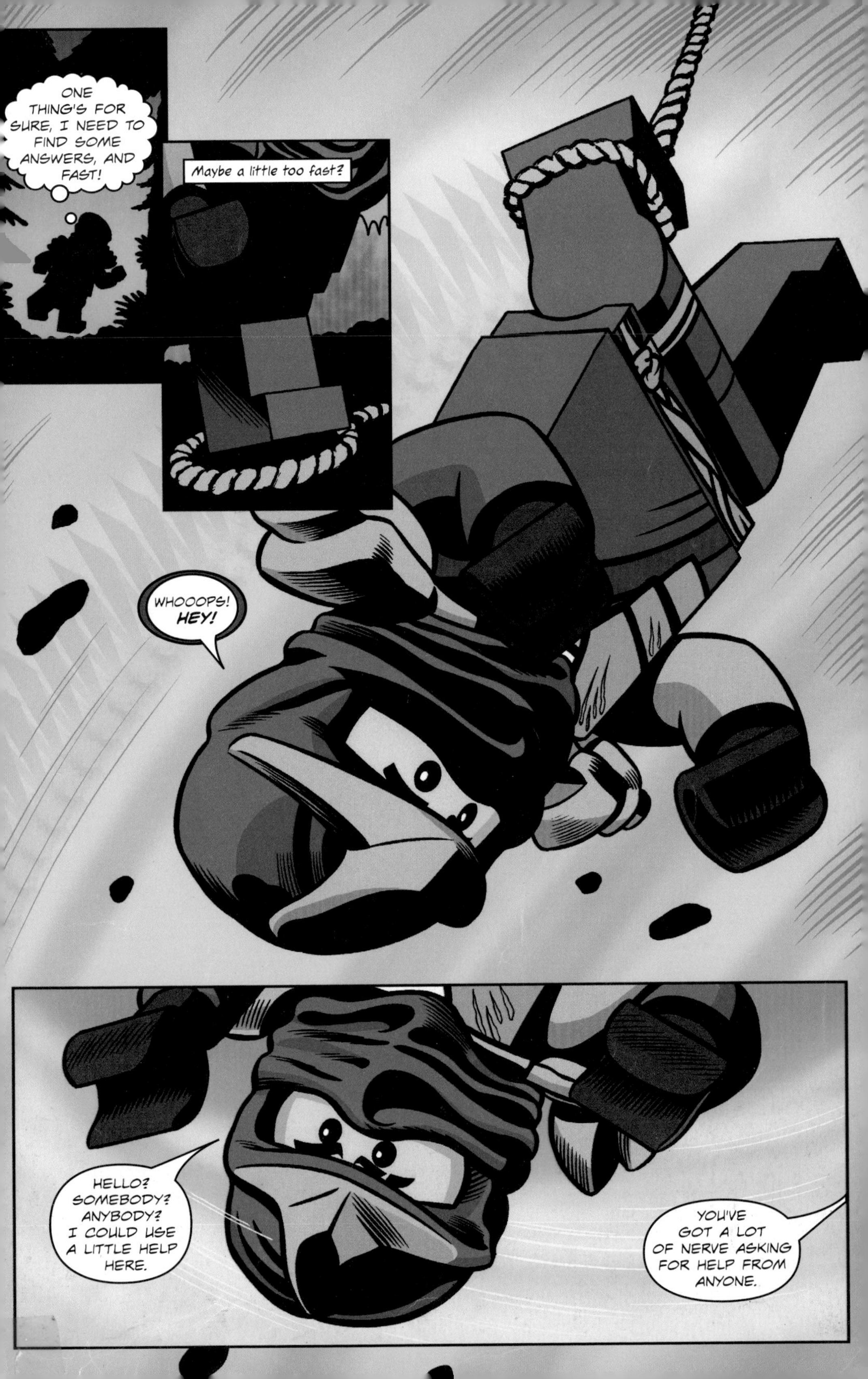
ONE THING'S FOR SURE, I NEED TO FIND SOME ANSWERS, AND FAST!
Maybe a little too fast?
WHOOOPS! HEY!
HELLO? SOMEBODY? ANYBODY? I COULD USE A LITTLE HELP HERE.
YOU'VE GOT A LOT OF NERVE ASKING FOR HELP FROM ANYONE.

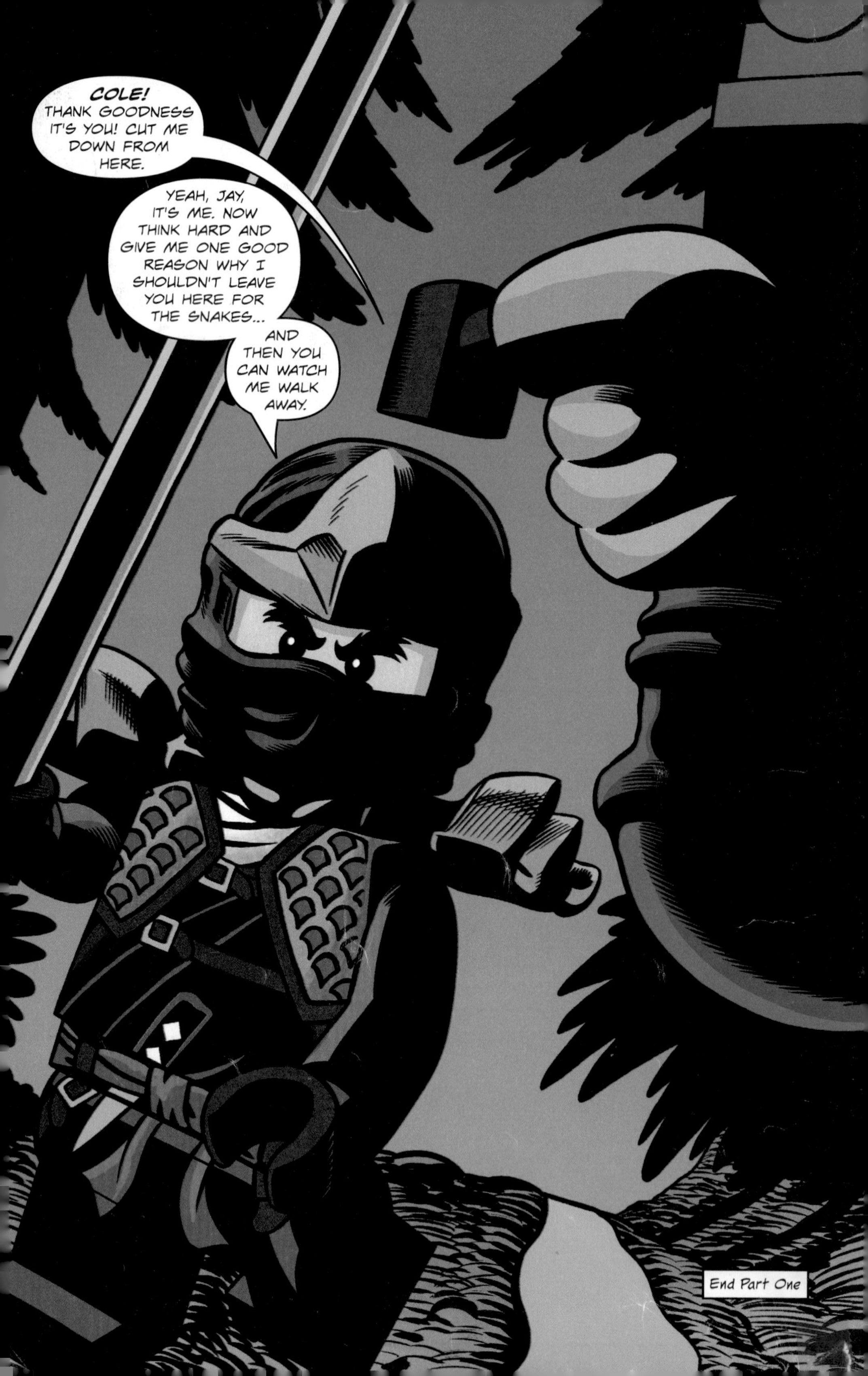
COLE! THANK GOODNESS IT'S YOU! CUT ME DOWN FROM HERE.
YEAH, JAY, IT'S ME. NOW THINK HARD AND GIVE ME ONE GOOD REASON WHY I SHOULDN'T LEAVE YOU HERE FOR THE SNAKES...
AND THEN YOU CAN WATCH ME WALK AWAY.
End Part One

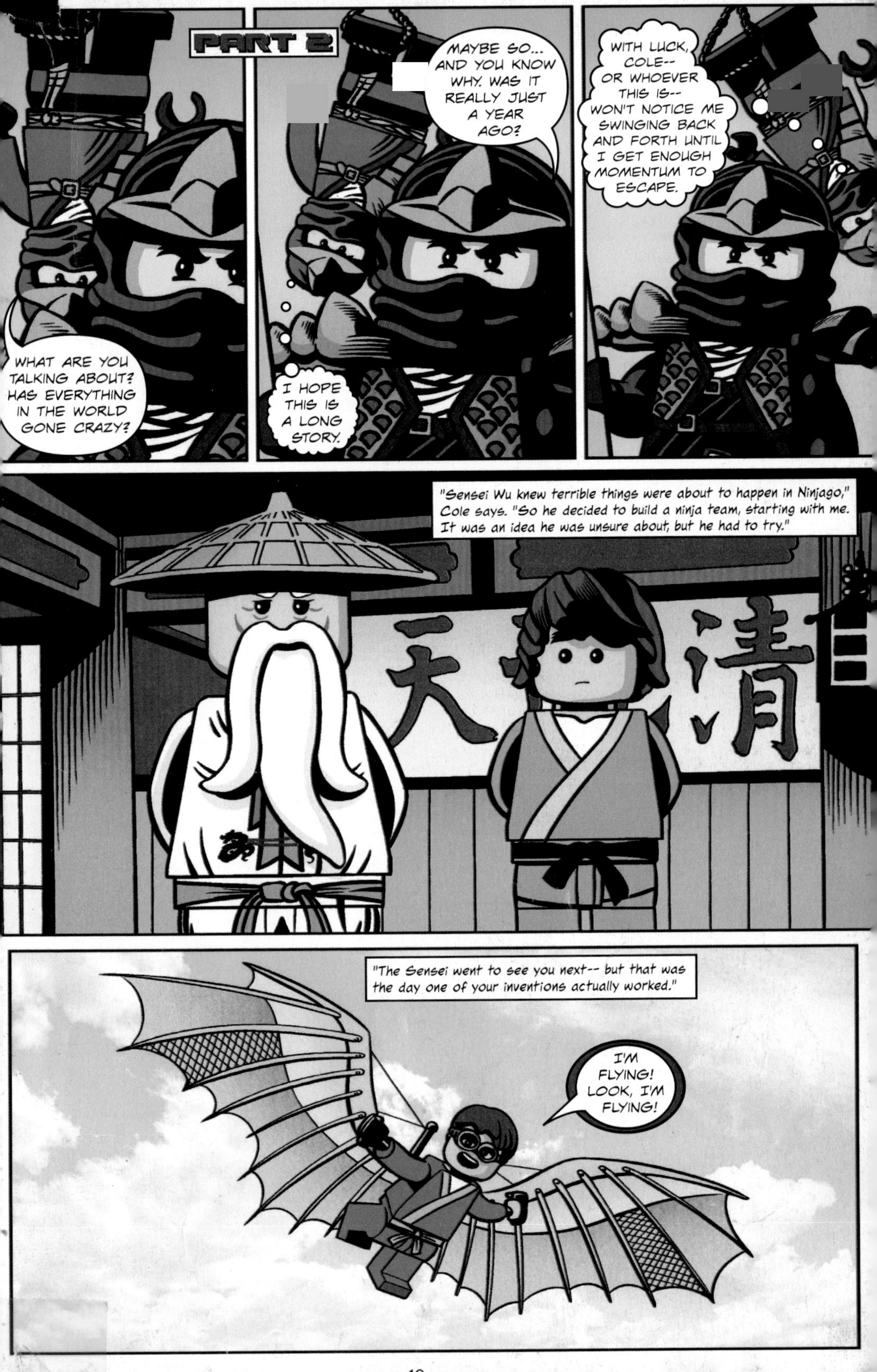
PART 2
WHAT ARE YOU TALKING ABOUT? HAS EVERYTHING IN THE WORLD GONE CRAZY?
MAYBE SO... AND YOU KNOW WHY. WAS IT REALLY JUST A YEAR AGO?
I HOPE THIS IS A LONG STORY.
WITH LUCK, COLE-- OR WHOEVER THIS IS-- WON'T NOTICE ME SWINGING BACK AND FORTH UNTIL I GET ENOUGH MOMENTUM TO ESCAPE.
"Sensei Wu knew terrible things were about to happen in Ninjago," Cole says. "So he decided to build a ninja team, starting with me. It was an idea he was unsure about, but he had to try."
"The Sensei went to see you next-- but that was the day one of your inventions actually worked."
I'M FLYING! LOOK, I'M FLYING!

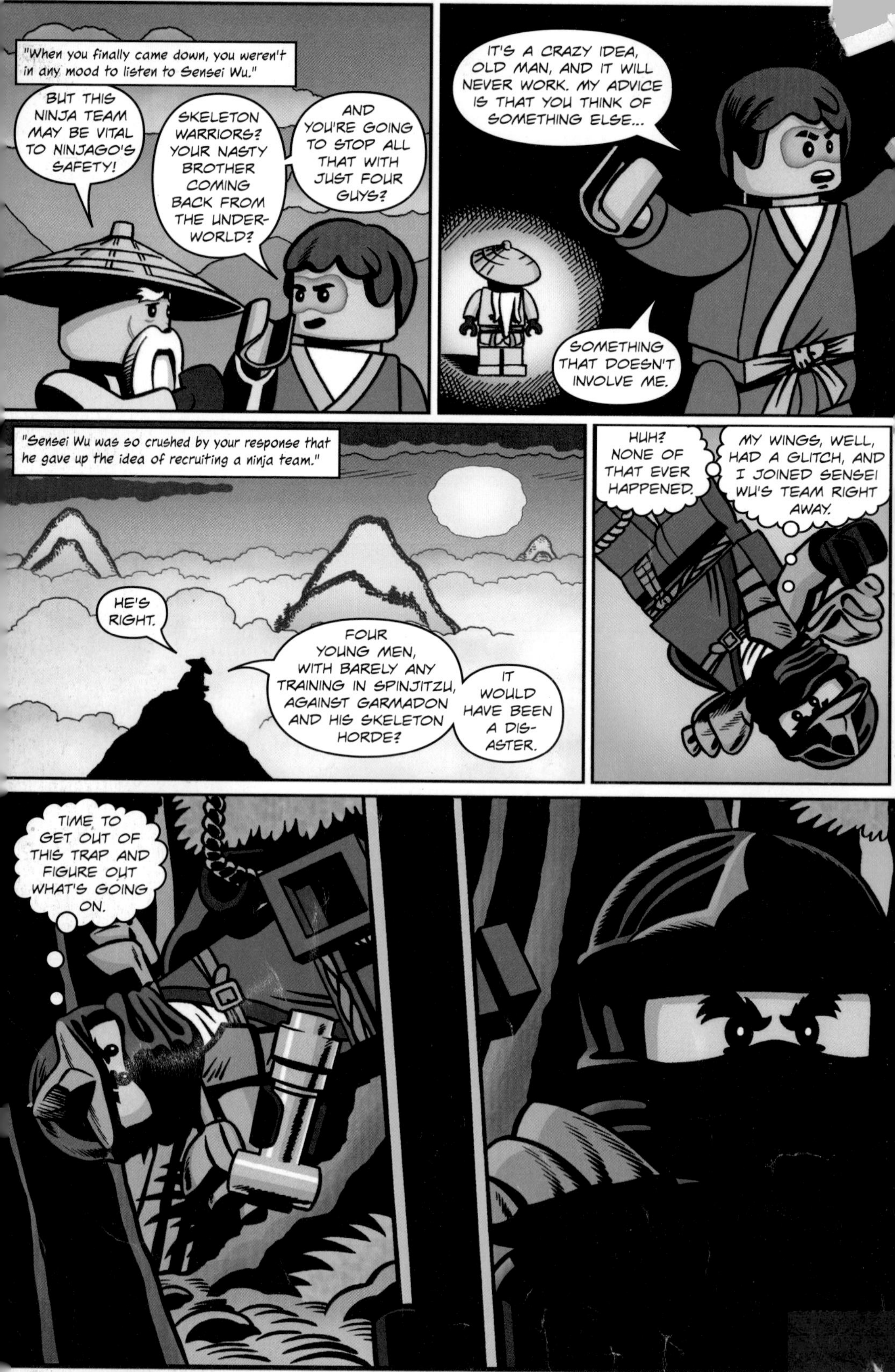
"When you finally came down, you weren't in any mood to listen to Sensei Wu."
BUT THIS NINJA TEAM MAY BE VITAL TO NINJAGO'S SAFETY!
SKELETON WARRIORS? YOUR NASTY BROTHER COMING BACK FROM THE UNDER-WORLD?
AND YOU'RE GOING TO STOP ALL THAT WITH JUST FOUR GUYS?
IT'S A CRAZY IDEA, OLD MAN, AND IT WILL NEVER WORK. MY ADVICE IS THAT YOU THINK OF SOMETHING ELSE...
SOMETHING THAT DOESN'T INVOLVE ME.
"Sensei Wu was so crushed by your response that he gave up the idea of recruiting a ninja team."
HE'S RIGHT.
FOUR YOUNG MEN, WITH BARELY ANY TRAINING IN SPINJITZU, AGAINST GARMADON AND HIS SKELETON HORDE?
IT WOULD HAVE BEEN A DIS-ASTER.
HUH? NONE OF THAT EVER HAPPENED.
MY WINGS, WELL, HAD A GLITCH, AND I JOINED SENSEI WU'S TEAM RIGHT AWAY.
TIME TO GET OUT OF THIS TRAP AND FIGURE OUT WHAT'S GOING ON.

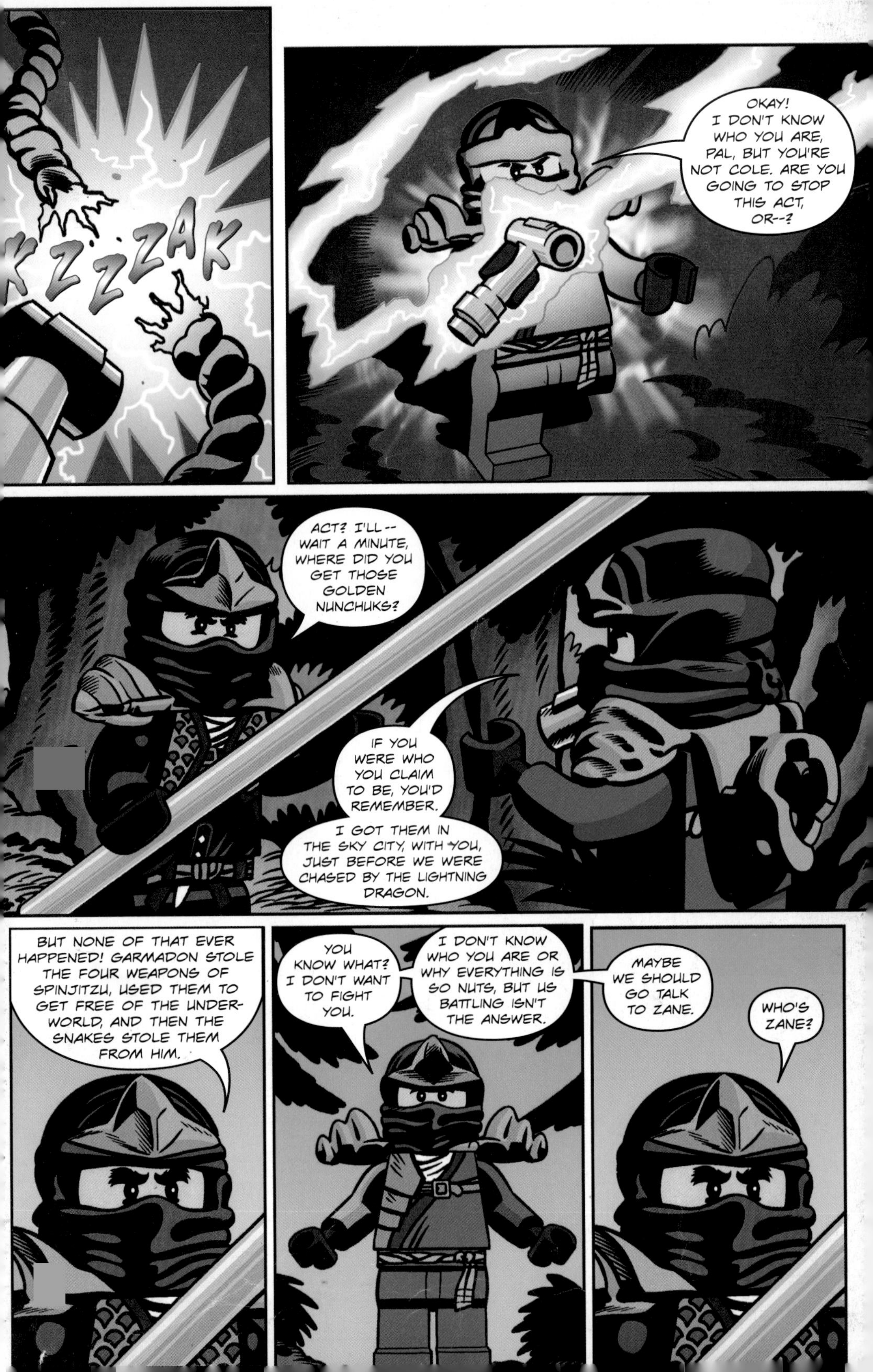
KZZZZAK
OKAY! I DON'T KNOW WHO YOU ARE, PAL, BUT YOU'RE NOT COLE. ARE YOU GOING TO STOP THIS ACT, OR--?
ACT? I'LL-- WAIT A MINUTE, WHERE DID YOU GET THOSE GOLDEN NUNCHUKS?
IF YOU WERE WHO YOU CLAIM TO BE, YOU'D REMEMBER.
I GOT THEM IN THE SKY CITY, WITH YOU, JUST BEFORE WE WERE CHASED BY THE LIGHTNING DRAGON.
BUT NONE OF THAT EVER HAPPENED! GARMADON STOLE THE FOUR WEAPONS OF SPINJITZU, USED THEM TO GET FREE OF THE UNDER-WORLD, AND THEN THE SNAKES STOLE THEM FROM HIM.
YOU KNOW WHAT? I DON'T WANT TO FIGHT YOU.
I DON'T KNOW WHO YOU ARE OR WHY EVERYTHING IS SO NUTS, BUT US BATTLING ISN'T THE ANSWER.
MAYBE WE SHOULD GO TALK TO ZANE.
WHO'S ZANE?

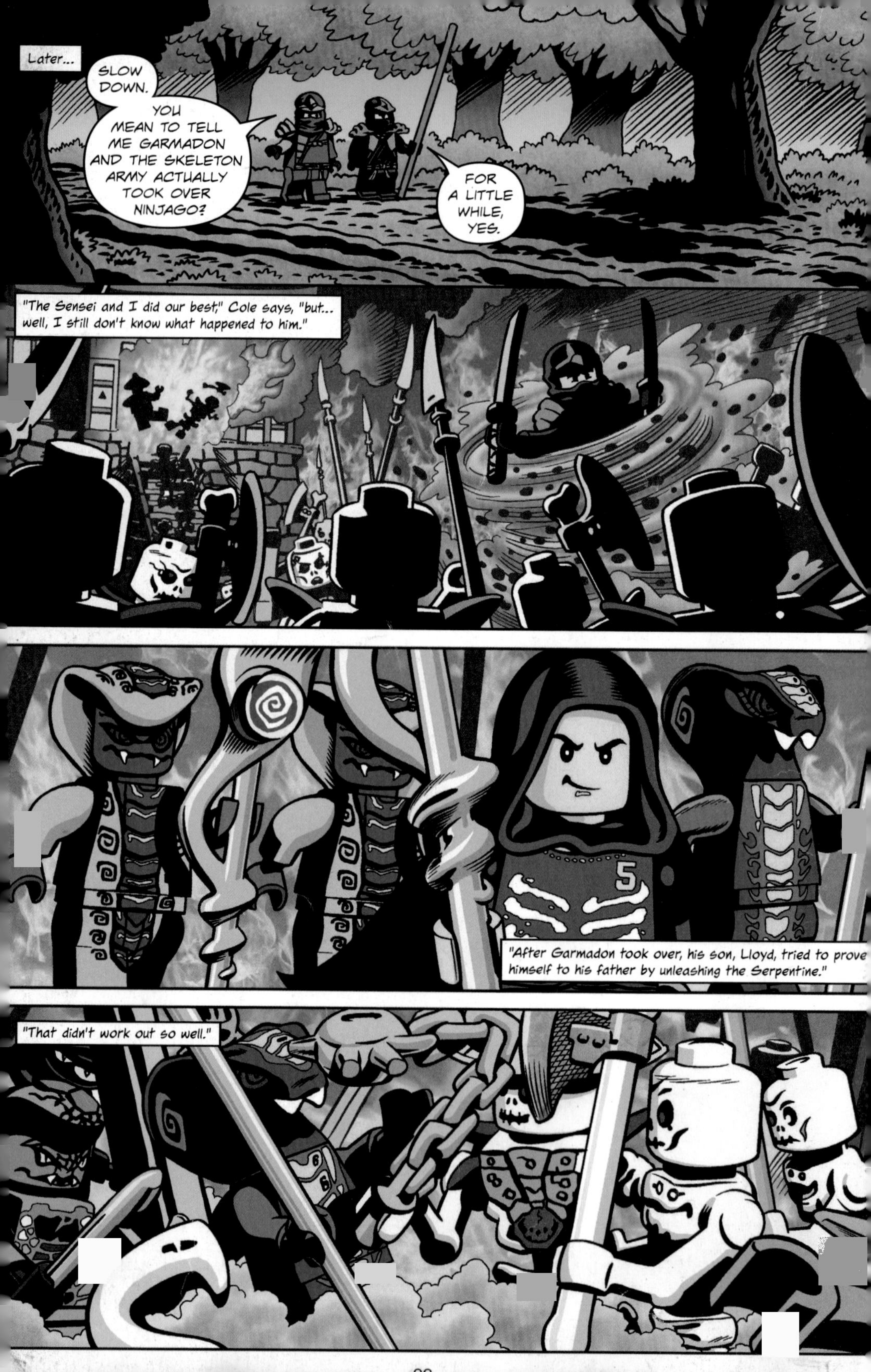
Later...
SLOW DOWN.
YOU MEAN TO TELL ME GARMADON AND THE SKELETON ARMY ACTUALLY TOOK OVER NINJAGO?
FOR A LITTLE WHILE, YES.
"The Sensei and I did our best," Cole says, "but... well, I still don't know what happened to him."
"After Garmadon took over, his son, Lloyd, tried to prove himself to his father by unleashing the Serpentine."
"That didn't work out so well."

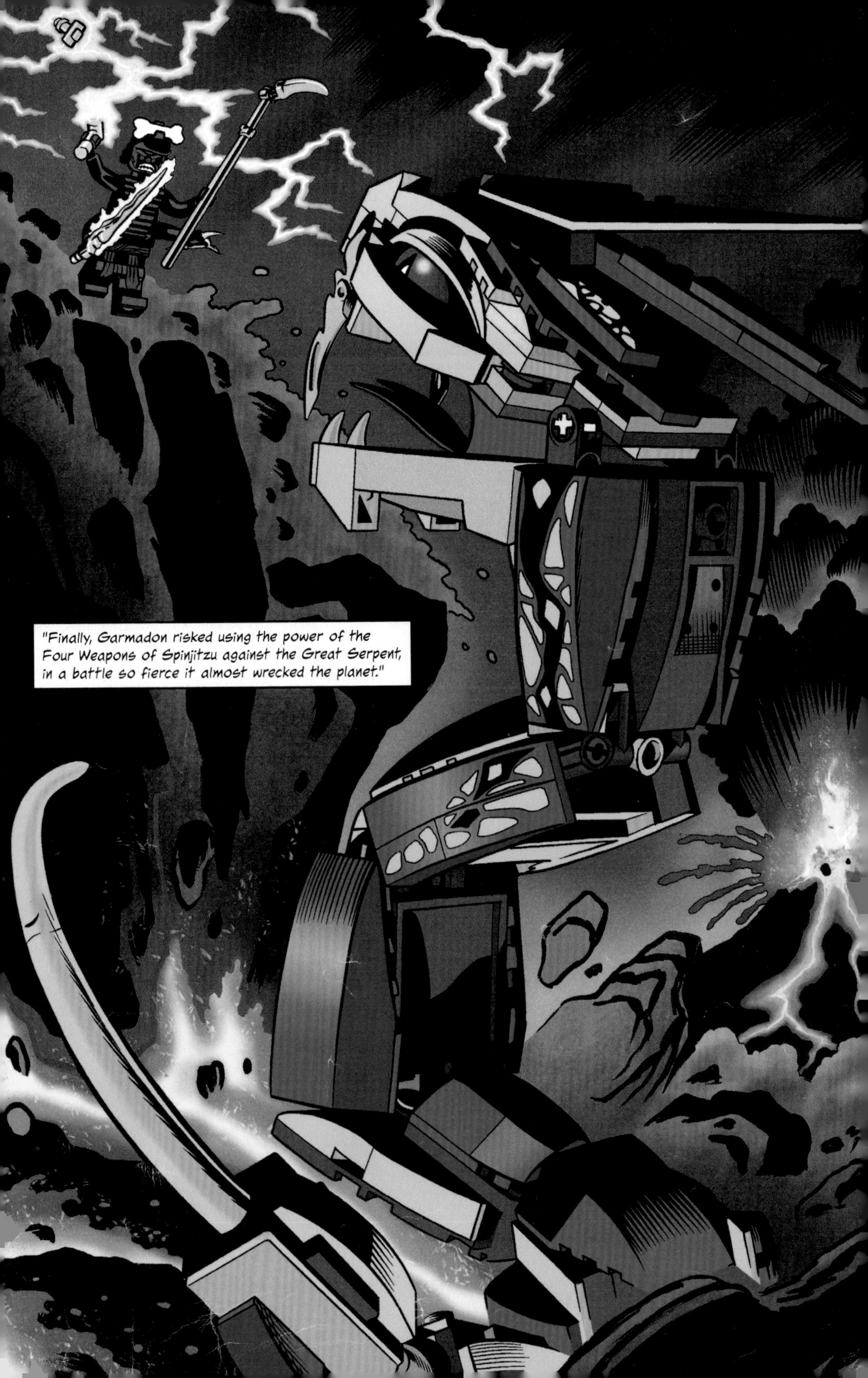
"Finally, Garmadon risked using the power of the Four Weapons of Spinjitzu against the Great Serpent, in a battle so fierce it almost wrecked the planet."

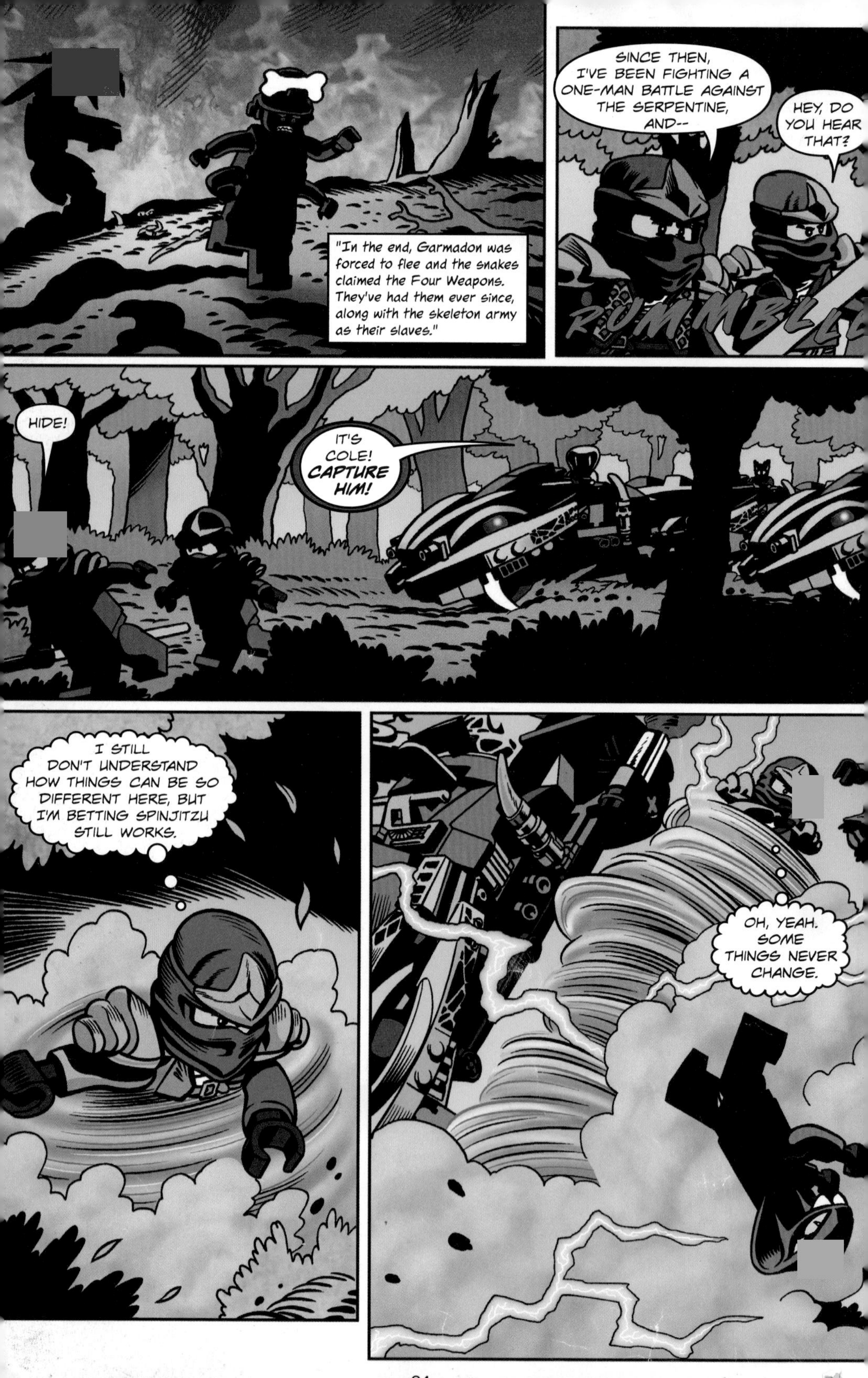
"In the end, Garmadon was forced to flee and the snakes claimed the Four Weapons. They've had them ever since, along with the skeleton army as their slaves."
SINCE THEN, I'VE BEEN FIGHTING A ONE-MAN BATTLE AGAINST THE SERPENTINE, AND--
HEY, DO YOU HEAR THAT?
RUMMBLLE
HIDE!
IT'S COLE! CAPTURE HIM!
I STILL DON'T UNDERSTAND HOW THINGS CAN BE SO DIFFERENT HERE, BUT I'M BETTING SPINJITZU STILL WORKS.
OH, YEAH. SOME THINGS NEVER CHANGE.

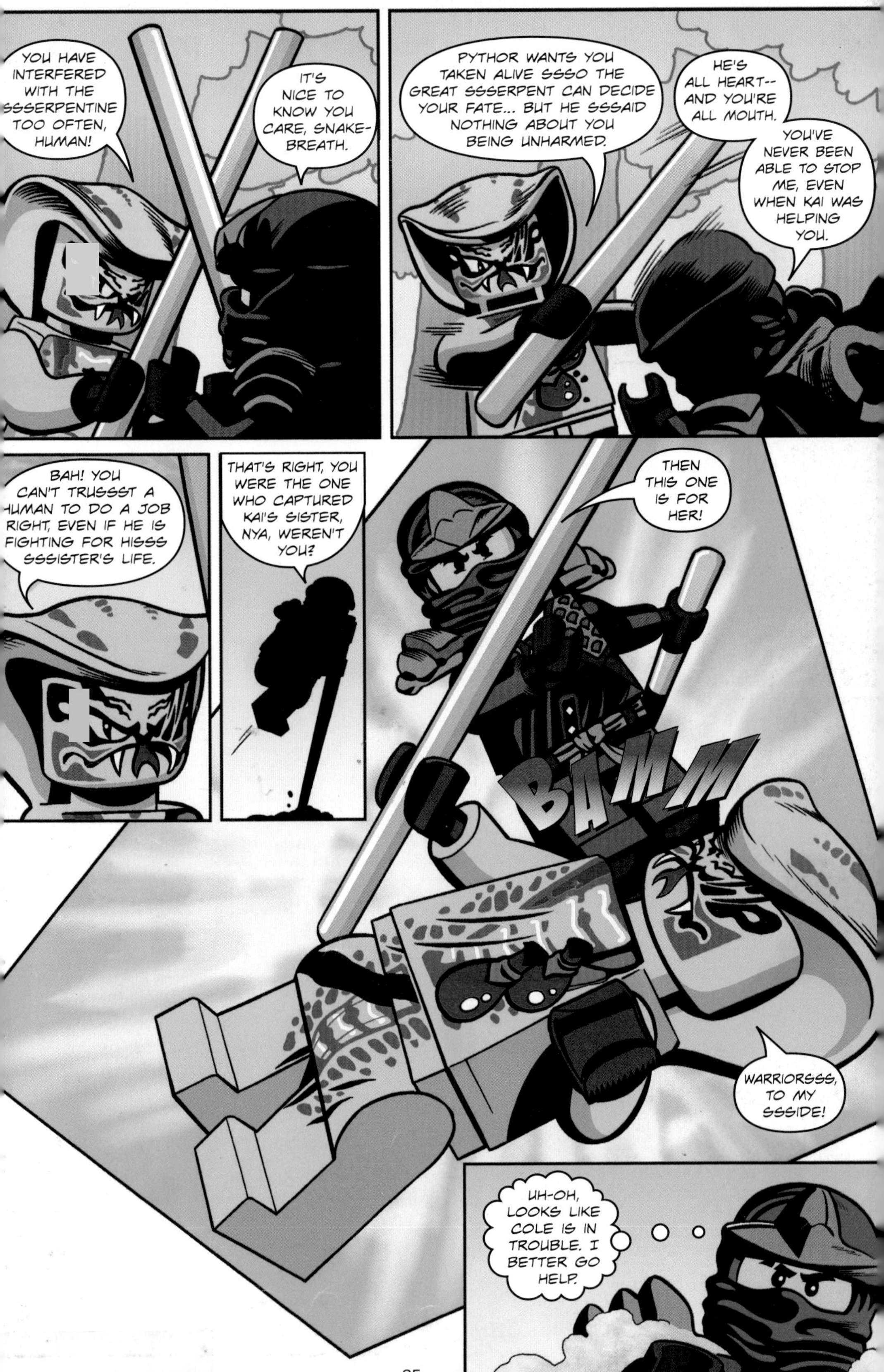
YOU HAVE INTERFERED WITH THE SSSERPENTINE TOO OFTEN, HUMAN!
IT'S NICE TO KNOW YOU CARE, SNAKE-BREATH.
PYTHOR WANTS YOU TAKEN ALIVE SSSO THE GREAT SSSERPENT CAN DECIDE YOUR FATE... BUT HE SSSAID NOTHING ABOUT YOU BEING UNHARMED.
HE'S ALL HEART-- AND YOU'RE ALL MOUTH.
YOU'VE NEVER BEEN ABLE TO STOP ME, EVEN WHEN KAI WAS HELPING YOU.
BAH! YOU CAN'T TRUSSST A HUMAN TO DO A JOB RIGHT, EVEN IF HE IS FIGHTING FOR HISSS SSSISTER'S LIFE.
THAT'S RIGHT, YOU WERE THE ONE WHO CAPTURED KAI'S SISTER, NYA, WEREN'T YOU?
THEN THIS ONE IS FOR HER!
BAMM
WARRIORSSS, TO MY SSSIDE!
UH-OH, LOOKS LIKE COLE IS IN TROUBLE. I BETTER GO HELP.

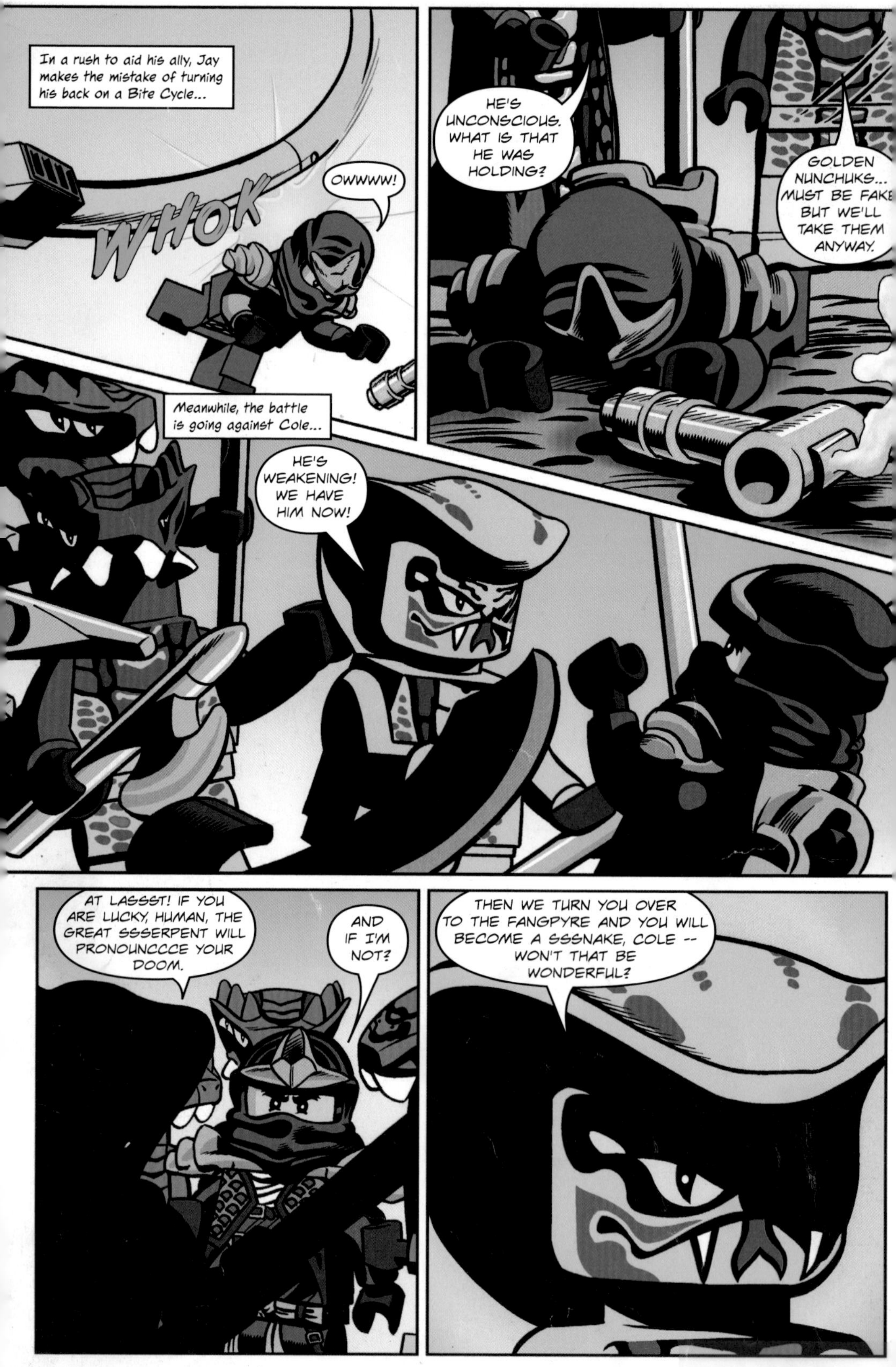

In a rush to aid his ally, Jay makes the mistake of turning his back on a Bite Cycle...
WHOK
OWWWW!
HE'S UNCONSCIOUS. WHAT IS THAT HE WAS HOLDING?
GOLDEN NUNCHUKS... MUST BE FAKE BUT WE'LL TAKE THEM ANYWAY.
Meanwhile, the battle is going against Cole...
HE'S WEAKENING! WE HAVE HIM NOW!
AT LASSST! IF YOU ARE LUCKY, HUMAN, THE GREAT SSSERPENT WILL PRONOUNCCCE YOUR DOOM.
AND IF I'M NOT?
THEN WE TURN YOU OVER TO THE FANGPYRE AND YOU WILL BECOME A SSSNAKE, COLE -- WON'T THAT BE WONDERFUL?

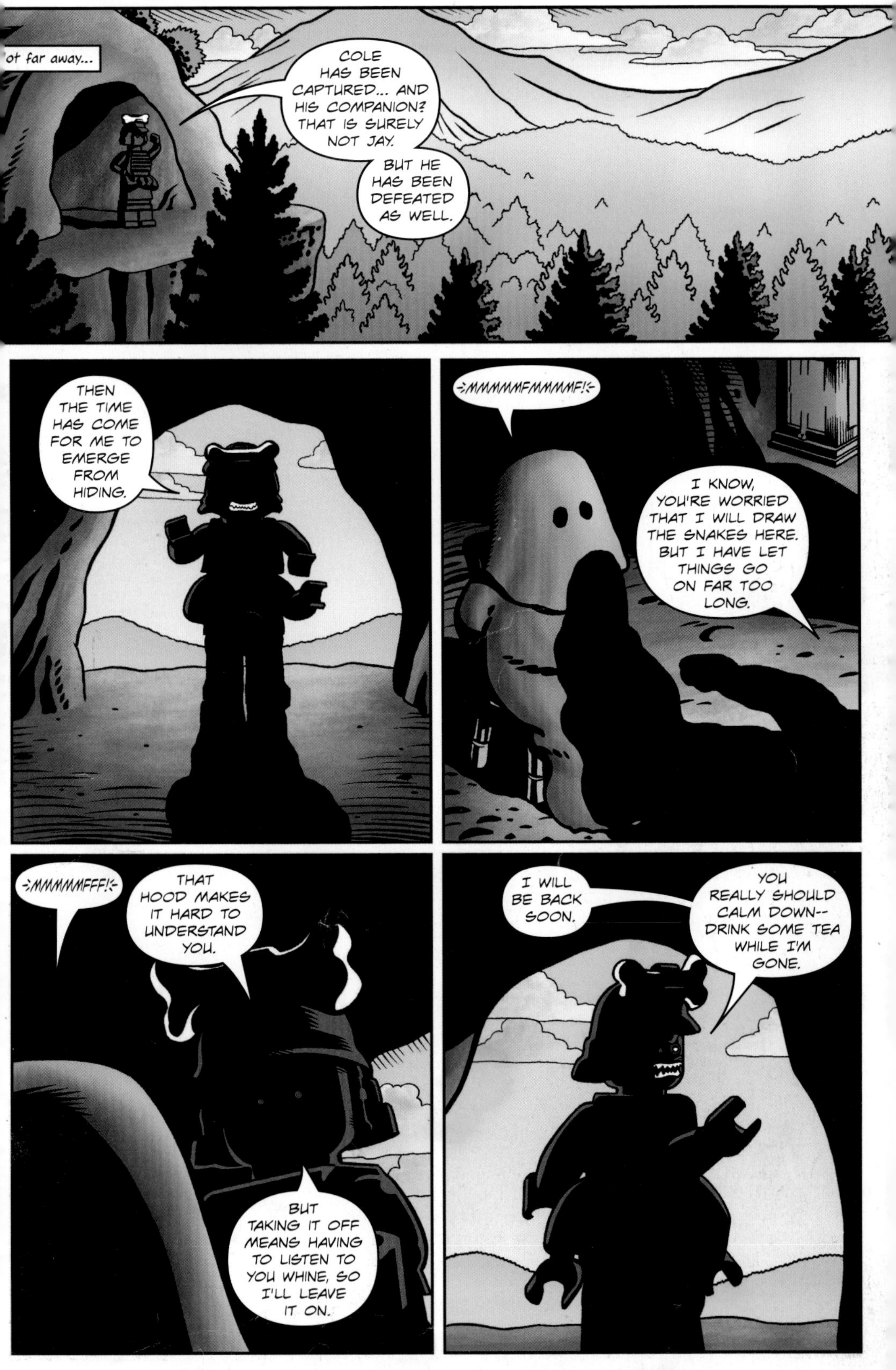
ot far away...
COLE HAS BEEN CAPTURED... AND HIS COMPANION? THAT IS SURELY NOT JAY.
BUT HE HAS BEEN DEFEATED AS WELL.
THEN THE TIME HAS COME FOR ME TO EMERGE FROM HIDING.
MMMMMFMMMMF!
I KNOW, YOU'RE WORRIED THAT I WILL DRAW THE SNAKES HERE. BUT I HAVE LET THINGS GO ON FAR TOO LONG.
MMMMMMFFF!
THAT HOOD MAKES IT HARD TO UNDERSTAND YOU.
BUT TAKING IT OFF MEANS HAVING TO LISTEN TO YOU WHINE, SO I'LL LEAVE IT ON.
I WILL BE BACK SOON.
YOU REALLY SHOULD CALM DOWN-- DRINK SOME TEA WHILE I'M GONE.

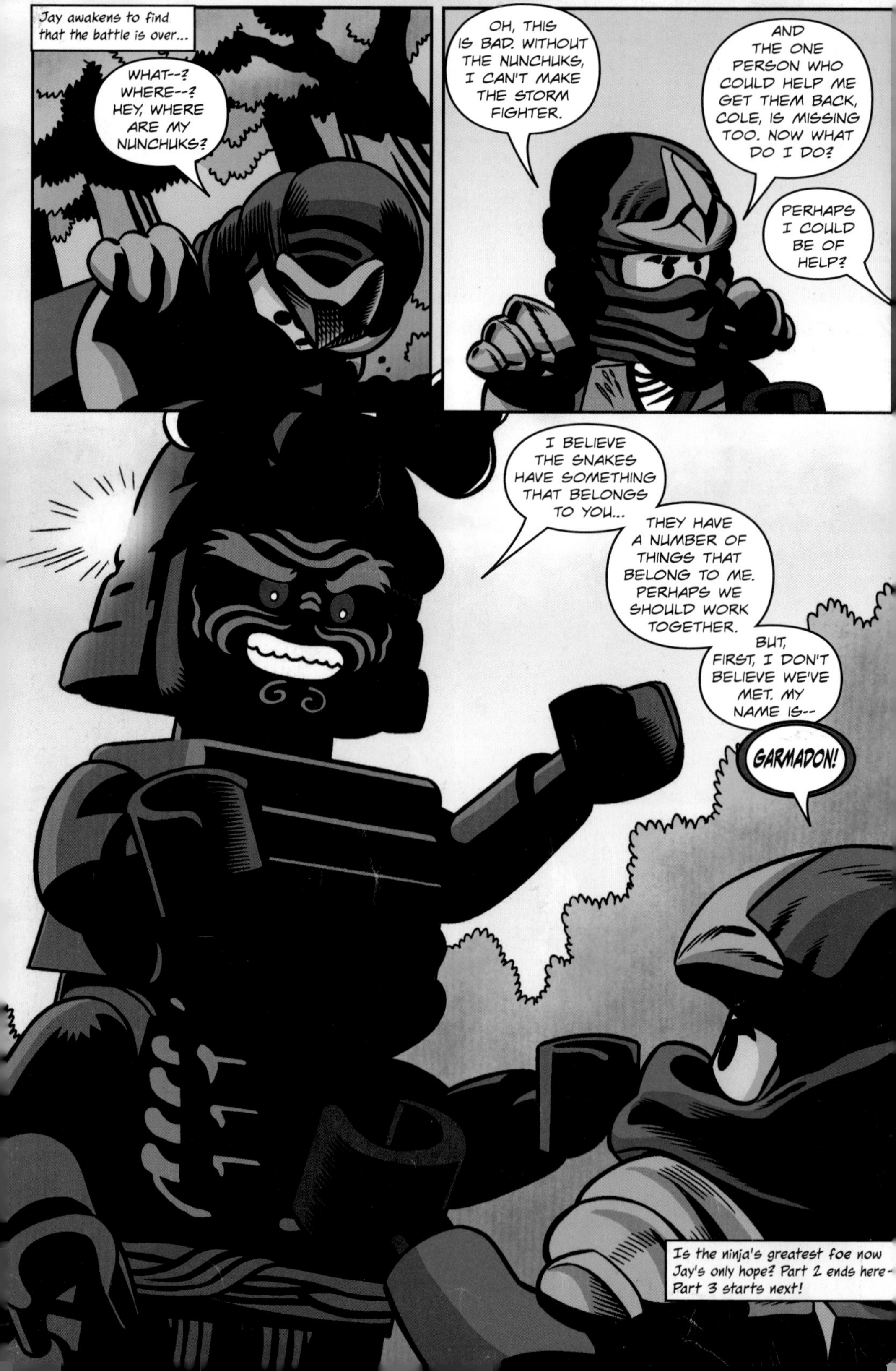

Jay awakens to find that the battle is over...
WHAT--? WHERE--? HEY, WHERE ARE MY NUNCHUKS?
OH, THIS IS BAD. WITHOUT THE NUNCHUKS, I CAN'T MAKE THE STORM FIGHTER.
AND THE ONE PERSON WHO COULD HELP ME GET THEM BACK, COLE, IS MISSING TOO. NOW WHAT DO I DO?
PERHAPS I COULD BE OF HELP?
I BELIEVE THE SNAKES HAVE SOMETHING THAT BELONGS TO YOU...
THEY HAVE A NUMBER OF THINGS THAT BELONG TO ME. PERHAPS WE SHOULD WORK TOGETHER.
BUT, FIRST, I DON'T BELIEVE WE'VE MET. MY NAME IS--
GARMADON!
Is the ninja's greatest foe now Jay's only hope? Part 2 ends here-Part 3 starts next!

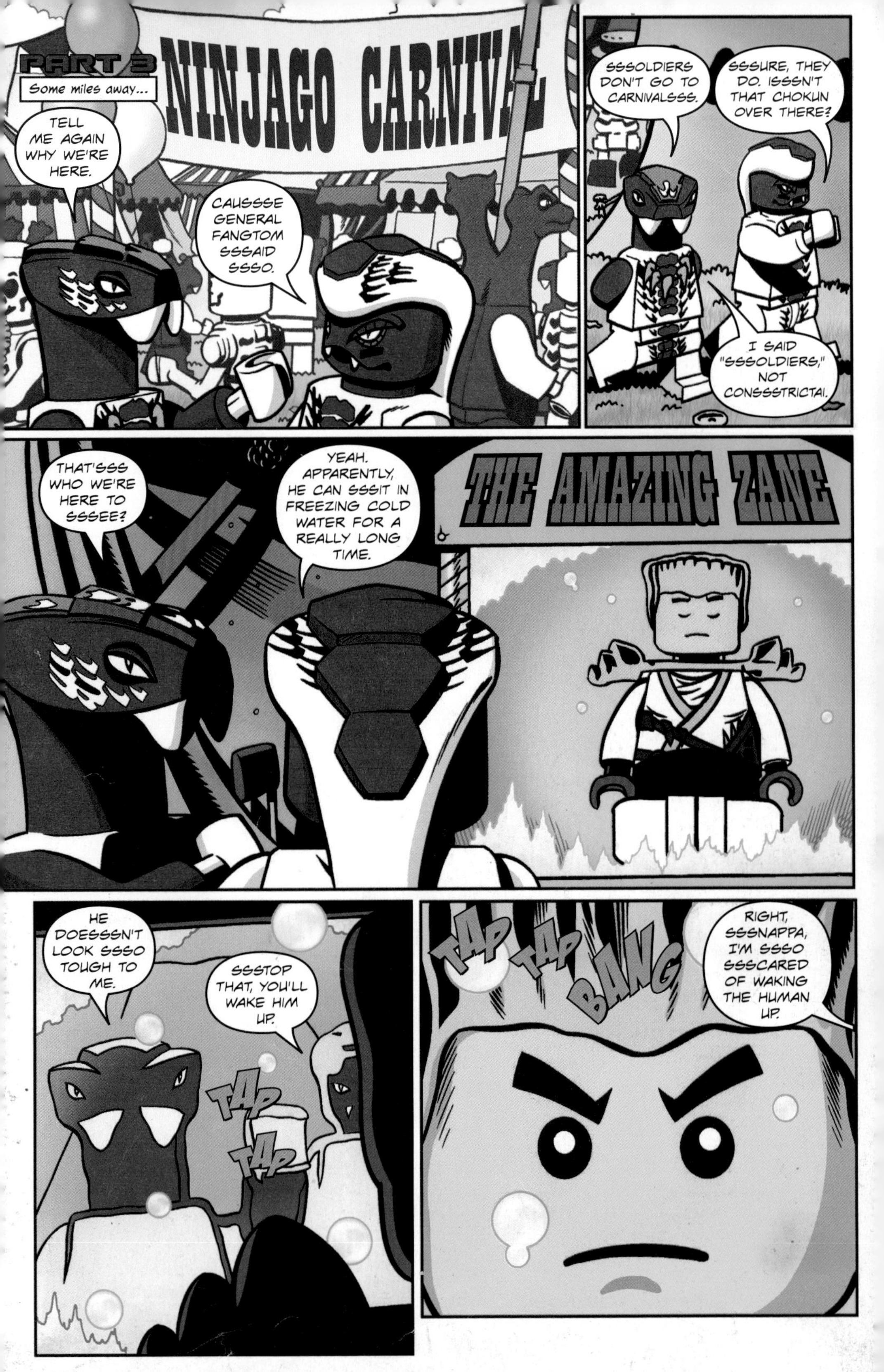
PART 3
NINJAGO CARNIVAL
Some miles away...
TELL ME AGAIN WHY WE'RE HERE.
CAUSSSE GENERAL FANGTOM SSSAID SSSO.
SSSOLDIERS DON'T GO TO CARNIVALSSS.
SSSURE, THEY DO. ISSSN'T THAT CHOKUN OVER THERE?
I SAID "SSSOLDIERS," NOT CONSSSTRICTAI.
THAT'SSS WHO WE'RE HERE TO SSSEE?
YEAH. APPARENTLY, HE CAN SSSIT IN FREEZING COLD WATER FOR A REALLY LONG TIME.
THE AMAZING ZANE
HE DOESSSN'T LOOK SSSO TOUGH TO ME.
SSSTOP THAT, YOU'LL WAKE HIM UP.
TAP
TAP
TAP TAP BANG
RIGHT, SSSNAPPA, I'M SSSO SSSCARED OF WAKING THE HUMAN UP.

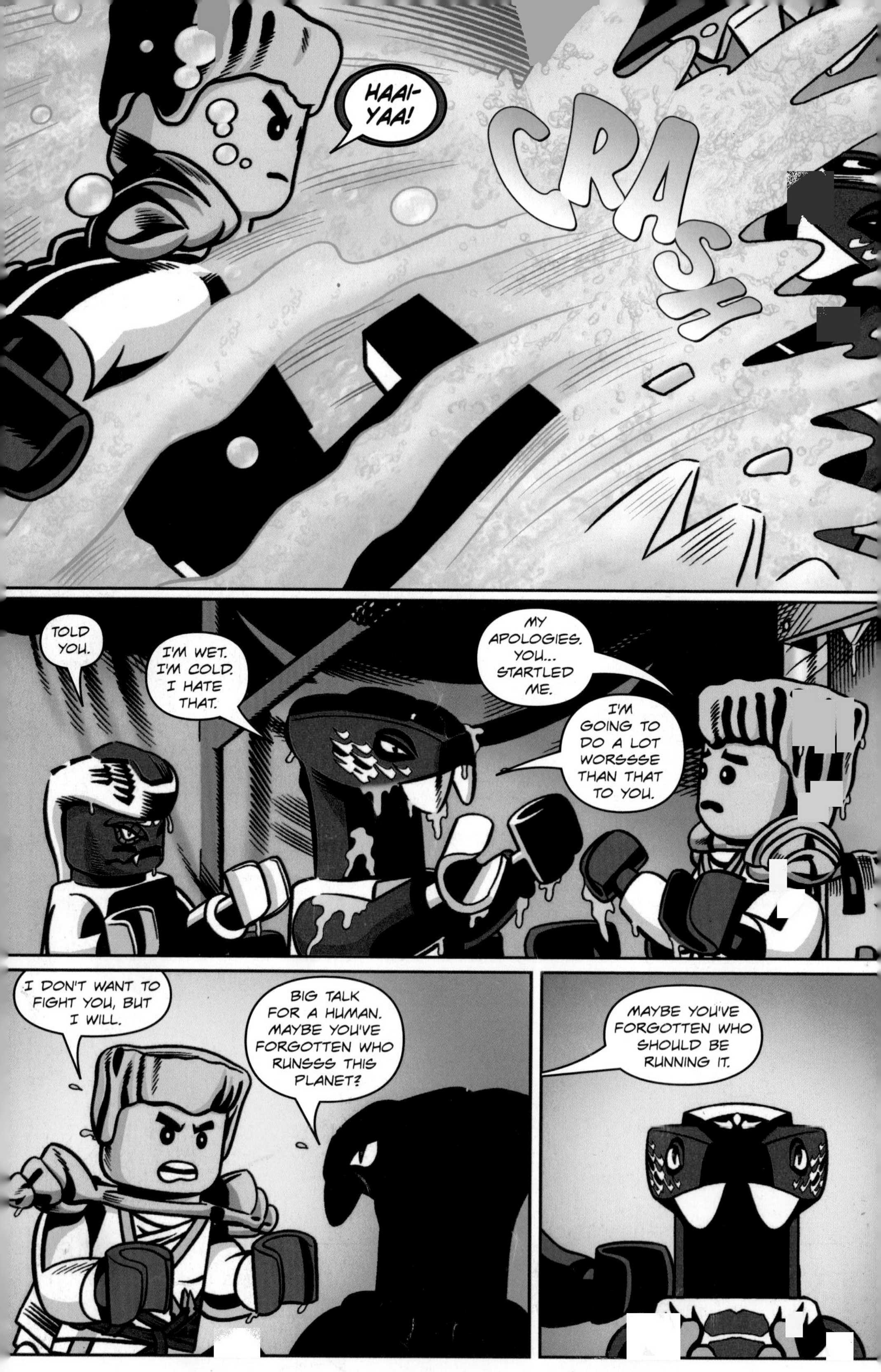
HAAI-YAA!
CRASH
TOLD YOU.
I'M WET. I'M COLD. I HATE THAT.
MY APOLOGIES. YOU... STARTLED ME.
I'M GOING TO DO A LOT WORSSSE THAN THAT TO YOU.
I DON'T WANT TO FIGHT YOU, BUT I WILL.
BIG TALK FOR A HUMAN. MAYBE YOU'VE FORGOTTEN WHO RUNSSS THIS PLANET?
MAYBE YOU'VE FORGOTTEN WHO SHOULD BE RUNNING IT.

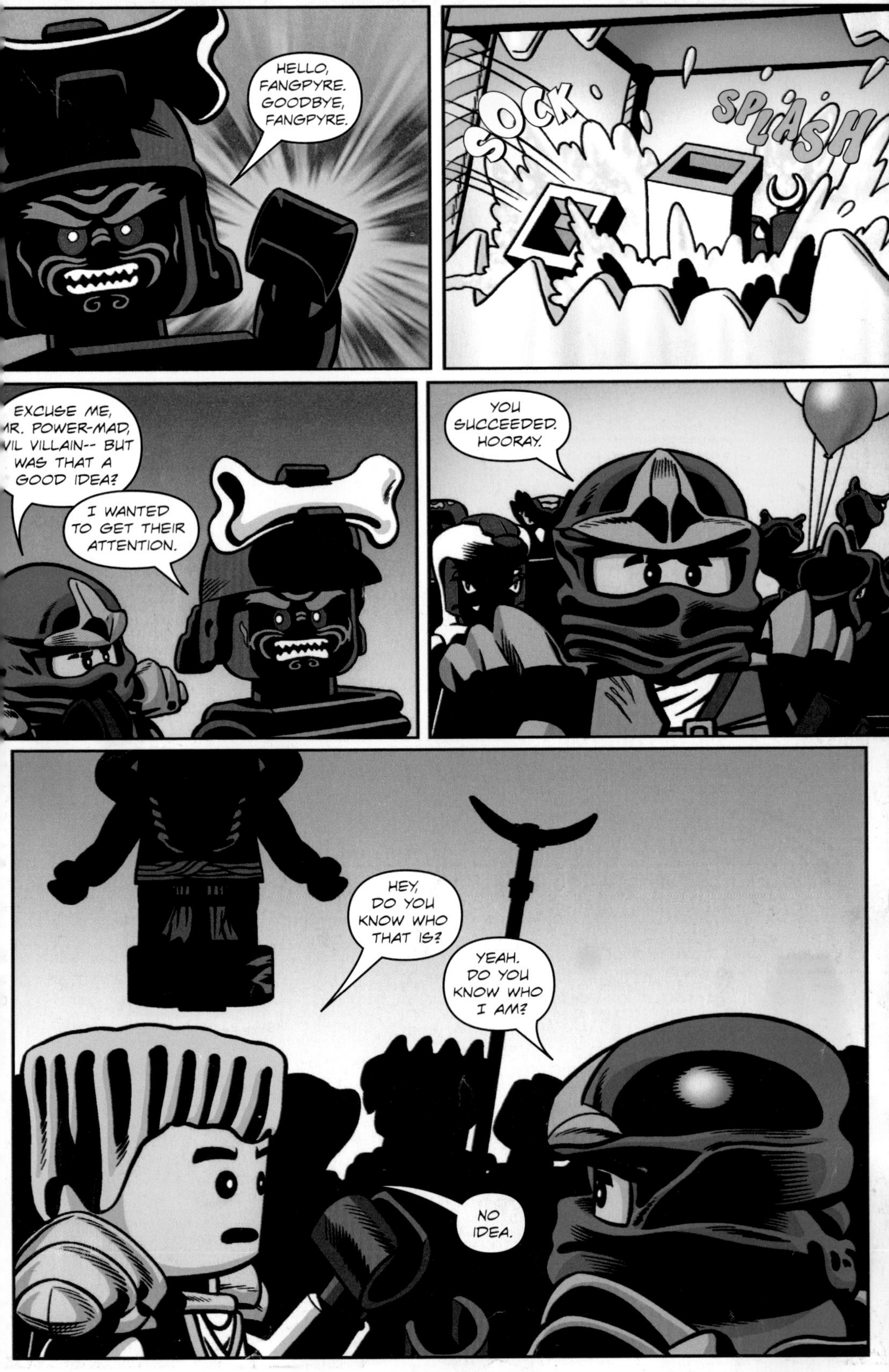
HELLO, FANGPYRE. GOODBYE, FANGPYRE.
SOCK
SPLASH
EXCUSE ME, MR. POWER-MAD, EVIL VILLAIN-- BUT WAS THAT A GOOD IDEA?
I WANTED TO GET THEIR ATTENTION.
YOU SUCCEEDED. HOORAY.
HEY, DO YOU KNOW WHO THAT IS?
YEAH. DO YOU KNOW WHO I AM?
NO IDEA.

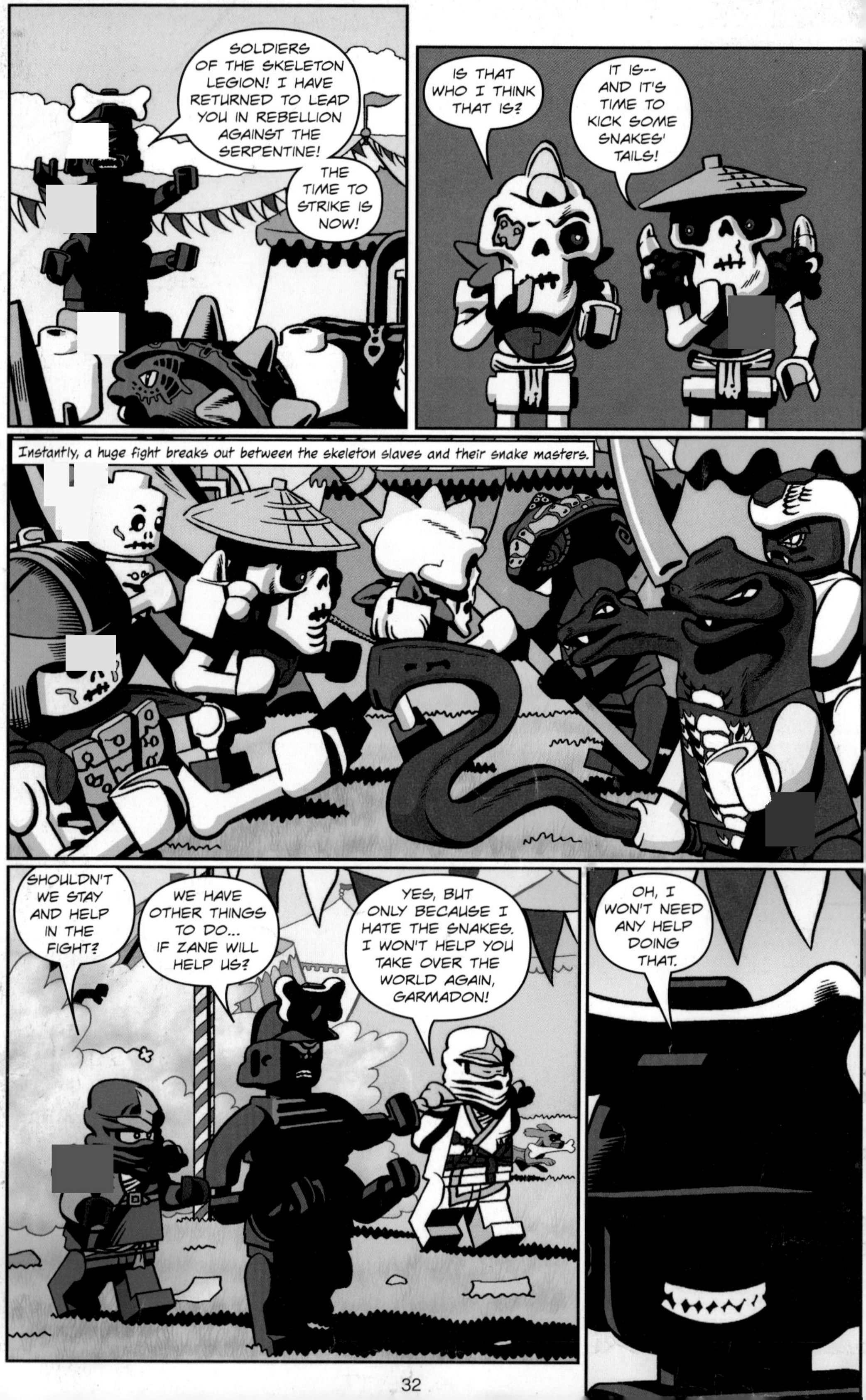
SOLDIERS OF THE SKELETON LEGION! I HAVE RETURNED TO LEAD YOU IN REBELLION AGAINST THE SERPENTINE!
THE TIME TO STRIKE IS NOW!
IS THAT WHO I THINK THAT IS?
IT IS-- AND IT'S TIME TO KICK SOME SNAKES' TAILS!
Instantly, a huge fight breaks out between the skeleton slaves and their snake masters.
SHOULDN'T WE STAY AND HELP IN THE FIGHT?
WE HAVE OTHER THINGS TO DO... IF ZANE WILL HELP US?
YES, BUT ONLY BECAUSE I HATE THE SNAKES. I WON'T HELP YOU TAKE OVER THE WORLD AGAIN, GARMADON!
OH, I WON'T NEED ANY HELP DOING THAT.

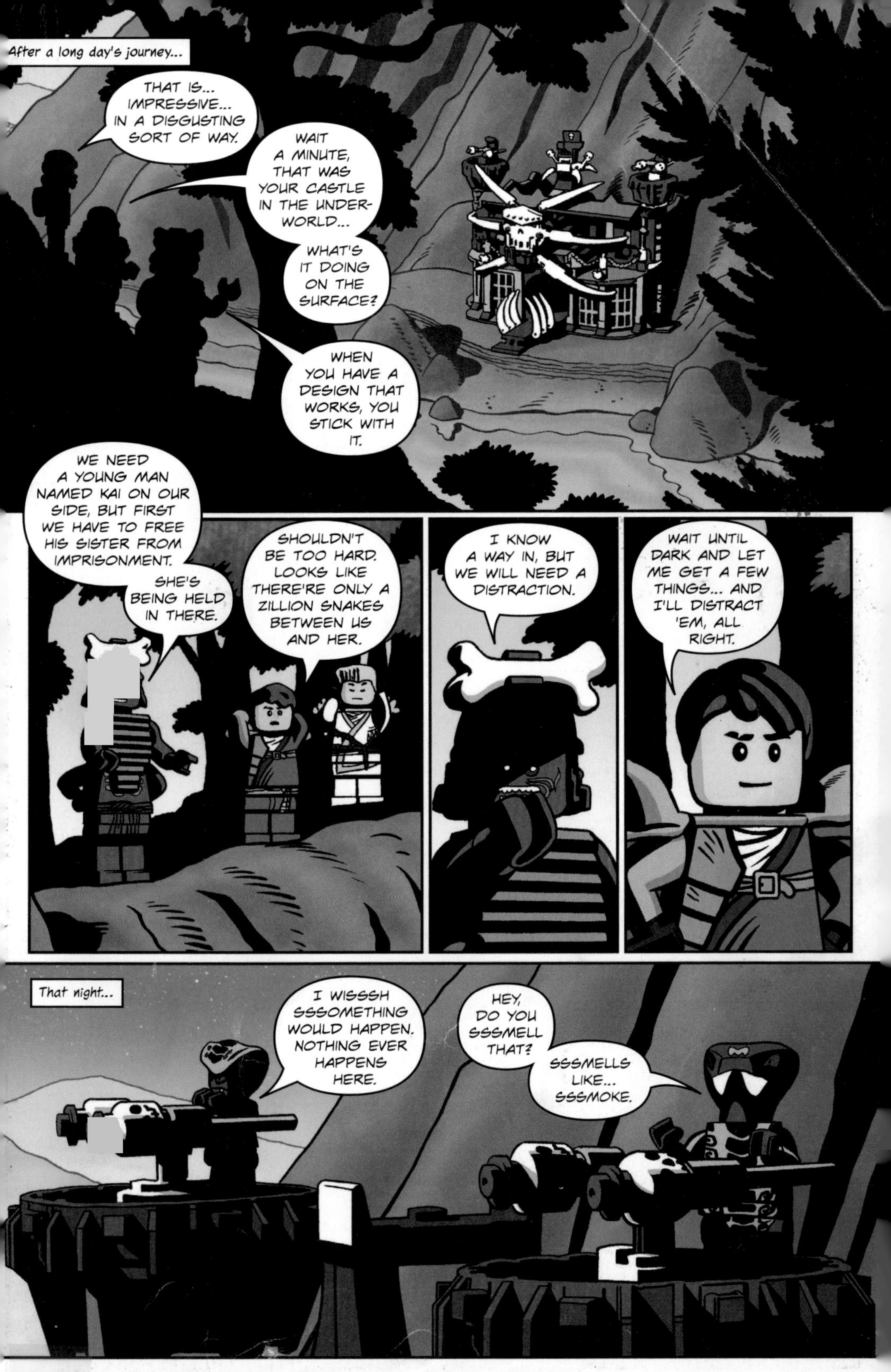
After a long day's journey...
THAT IS... IMPRESSIVE... IN A DISGUSTING SORT OF WAY.
WAIT A MINUTE, THAT WAS YOUR CASTLE IN THE UNDER-WORLD...
WHAT'S IT DOING ON THE SURFACE?
WHEN YOU HAVE A DESIGN THAT WORKS, YOU STICK WITH IT.
WE NEED A YOUNG MAN NAMED KAI ON OUR SIDE, BUT FIRST WE HAVE TO FREE HIS SISTER FROM IMPRISONMENT.
SHE'S BEING HELD IN THERE.
SHOULDN'T BE TOO HARD. LOOKS LIKE THERE'RE ONLY A ZILLION SNAKES BETWEEN US AND HER.
I KNOW A WAY IN, BUT WE WILL NEED A DISTRACTION.
WAIT UNTIL DARK AND LET ME GET A FEW THINGS... AND I'LL DISTRACT 'EM, ALL RIGHT.
That night...
I WISSSH SSSOMETHING WOULD HAPPEN. NOTHING EVER HAPPENS HERE.
HEY, DO YOU SSSMELL THAT?
SSSMELLS LIKE... SSSMOKE.

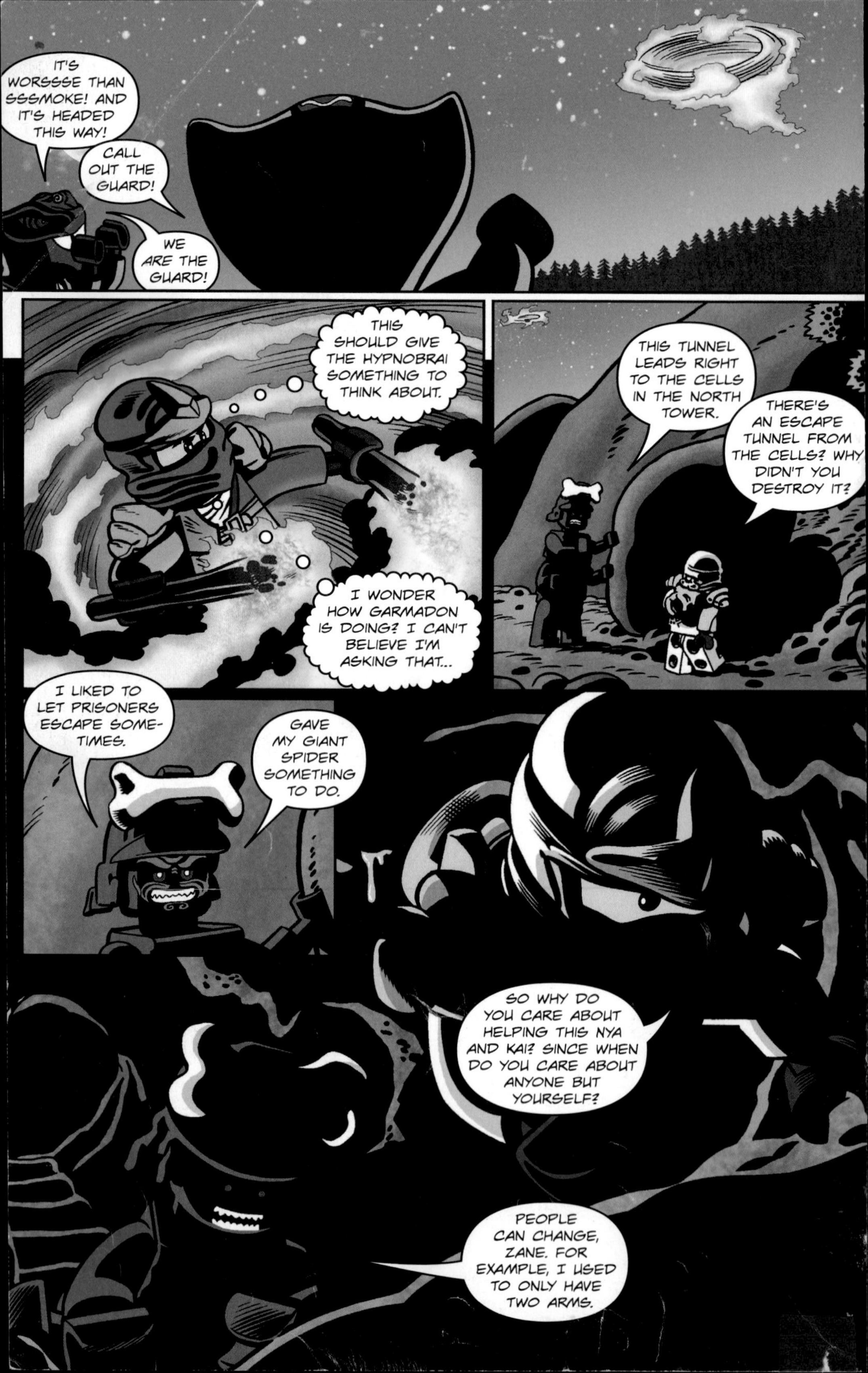
IT'S WORSSSE THAN SSSMOKE! AND IT'S HEADED THIS WAY!
CALL OUT THE GUARD!
WE ARE THE GUARD!
THIS SHOULD GIVE THE HYPNOBRAI SOMETHING TO THINK ABOUT.
I WONDER HOW GARMADON IS DOING? I CAN'T BELIEVE I'M ASKING THAT...
THIS TUNNEL LEADS RIGHT TO THE CELLS IN THE NORTH TOWER.
THERE'S AN ESCAPE TUNNEL FROM THE CELLS? WHY DIDN'T YOU DESTROY IT?
I LIKED TO LET PRISONERS ESCAPE SOME-TIMES.
GAVE MY GIANT SPIDER SOMETHING TO DO.
SO WHY DO YOU CARE ABOUT HELPING THIS NYA AND KAI? SINCE WHEN DO YOU CARE ABOUT ANYONE BUT YOURSELF?
PEOPLE CAN CHANGE, ZANE. FOR EXAMPLE, I USED TO ONLY HAVE TWO ARMS.

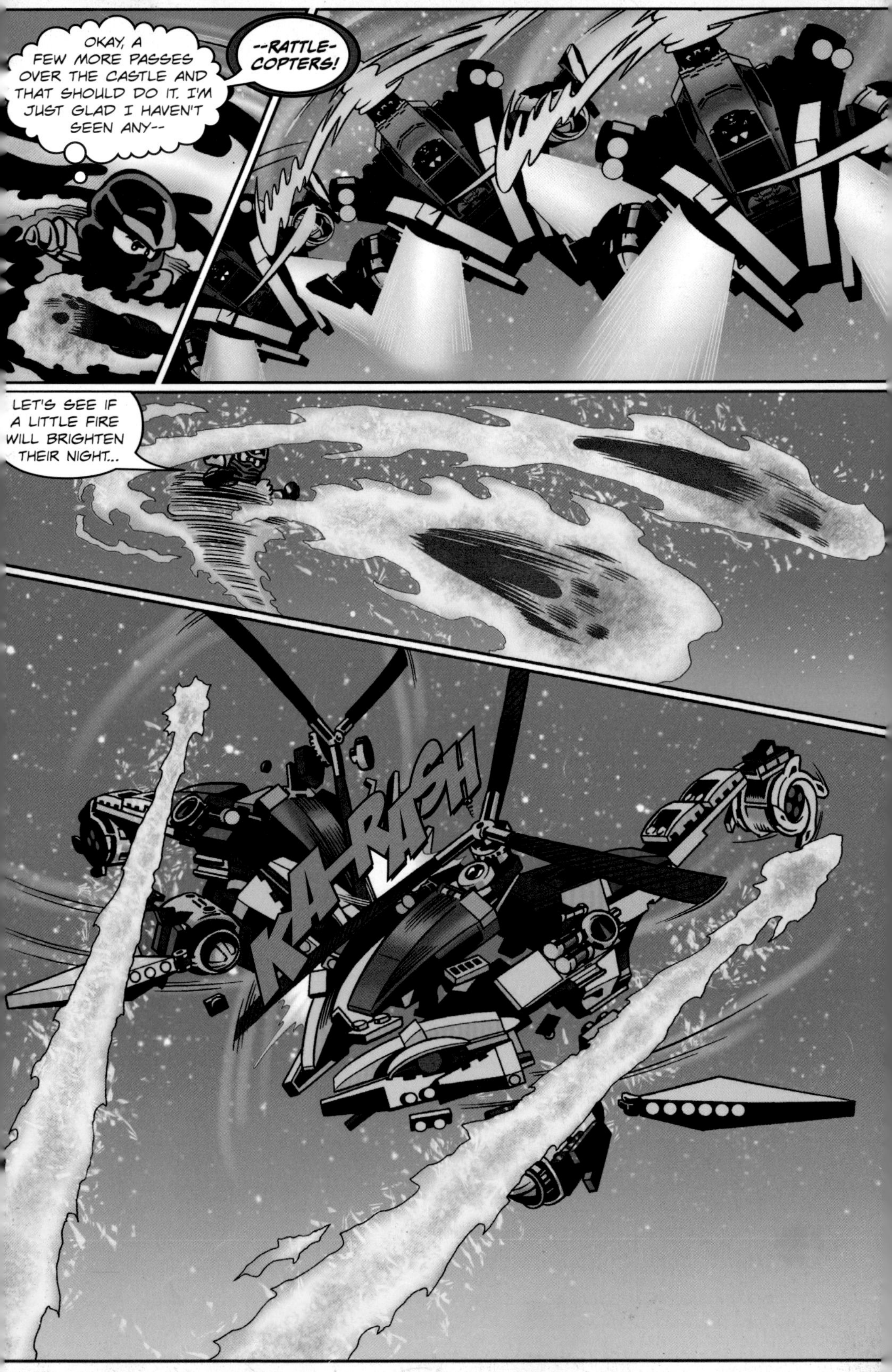
OKAY, A FEW MORE PASSES OVER THE CASTLE AND THAT SHOULD DO IT. I'M JUST GLAD I HAVEN'T SEEN ANY--
--RATTLE-COPTERS!
LET'S SEE IF A LITTLE FIRE WILL BRIGHTEN THEIR NIGHT...
KA-RASH

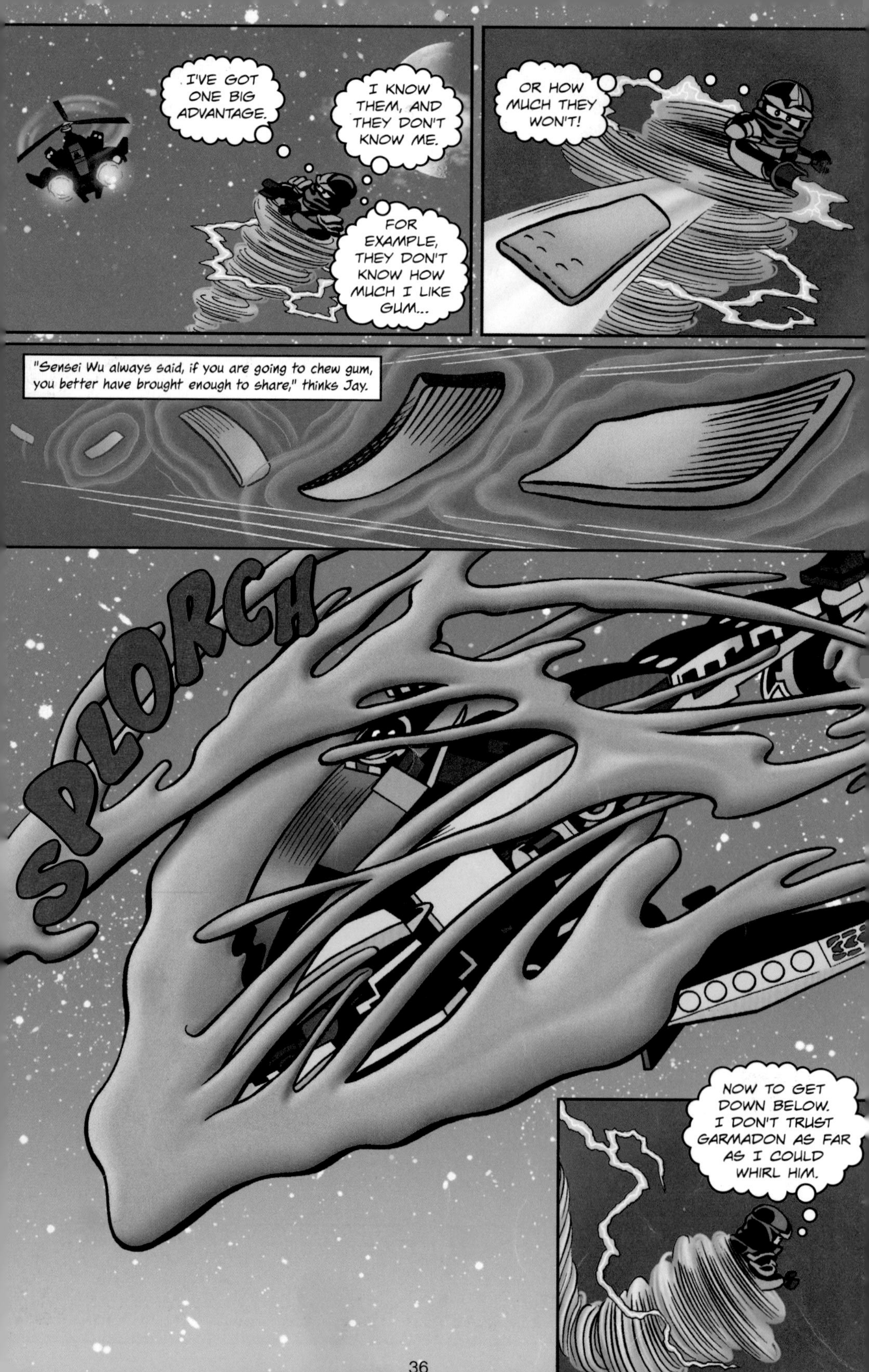
I'VE GOT ONE BIG ADVANTAGE.
I KNOW THEM, AND THEY DON'T KNOW ME.
FOR EXAMPLE, THEY DON'T KNOW HOW MUCH I LIKE GUM...
OR HOW MUCH THEY WON'T!
"Sensei Wu always said, if you are going to chew gum, you better have brought enough to share," thinks Jay.
SPLORCH
NOW TO GET DOWN BELOW. I DON'T TRUST GARMADON AS FAR AS I COULD WHIRL HIM.

WE'RE HERE.

HEY! WHO ARE YOU? HOW DID THAT TUNNEL GET THERE?

HOLD ON, I REMEMBER YOU-- YOU'RE GARMADON. WELL, YOU CAN JUST CLIMB BACK INTO WHATEVER HOLE YOU'VE BEEN LIVING IN, AND--

DO YOU ALWAYS TALK SO MUCH DURING A RESCUE?

IT'S TRUE. WE'RE HERE TO HELP YOU ESCAPE THE HYPNOBRAI.

YOU THINK I NEED HELP? HA!

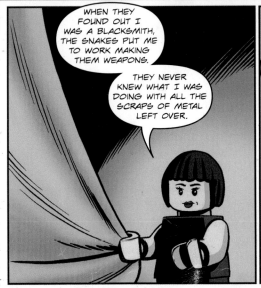

WHEN THEY FOUND OUT I WAS A BLACKSMITH, THE SNAKES PUT ME TO WORK MAKING THEM WEAPONS.

THEY NEVER KNEW WHAT I WAS DOING WITH ALL THE SCRAPS OF METAL LEFT OVER.

I'LL ESCAPE, ALL RIGHT, BUT NOT THROUGH A TUNNEL--

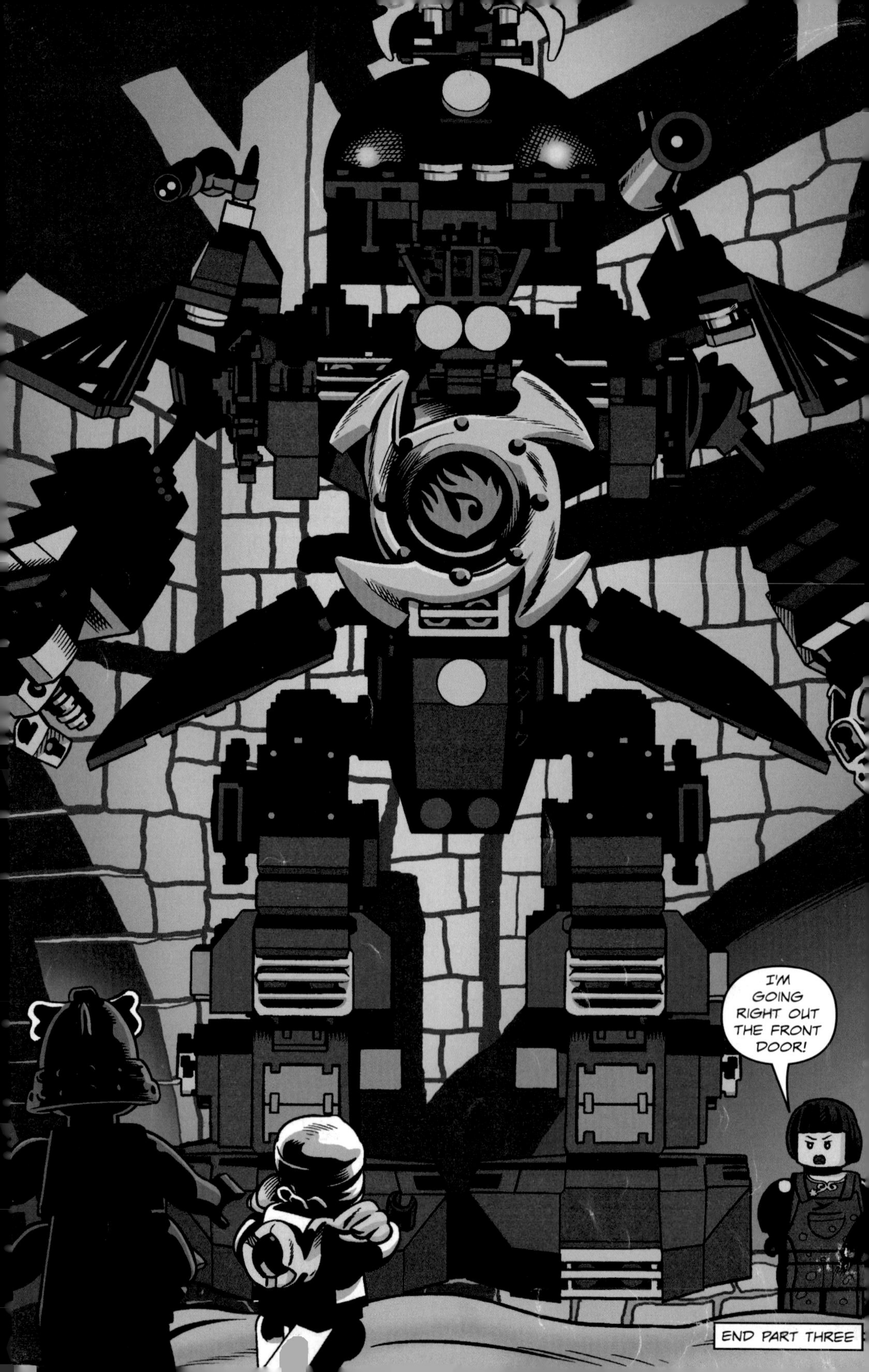
I'M GOING RIGHT OUT THE FRONT DOOR!
END PART THREE

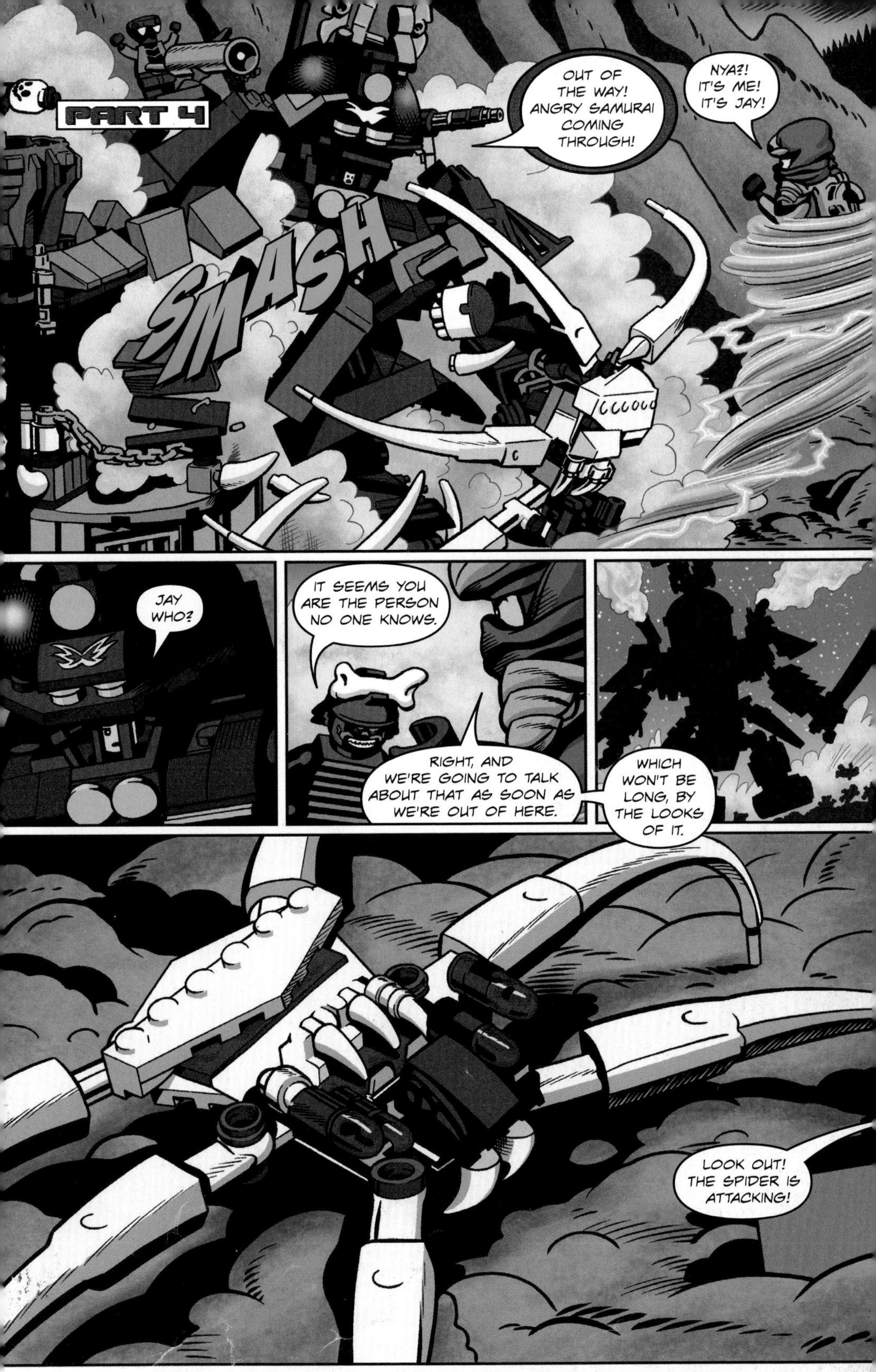
PART 4
OUT OF THE WAY! ANGRY SAMURAI COMING THROUGH!
NYA?! IT'S ME! IT'S JAY!
SMASH
JAY WHO?
IT SEEMS YOU ARE THE PERSON NO ONE KNOWS.
RIGHT, AND WE'RE GOING TO TALK ABOUT THAT AS SOON AS WE'RE OUT OF HERE.
WHICH WON'T BE LONG, BY THE LOOKS OF IT.
LOOK OUT! THE SPIDER IS ATTACKING!

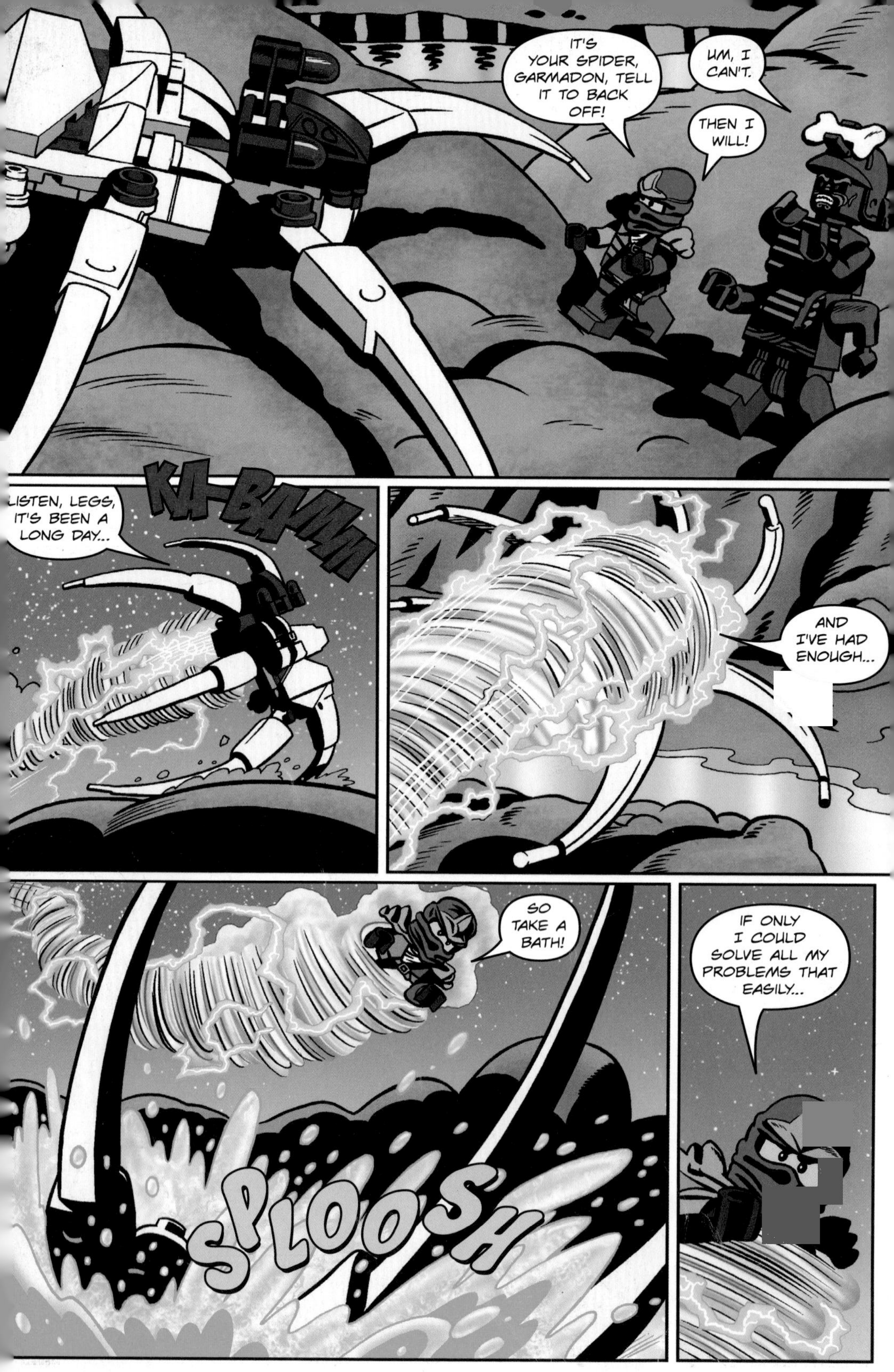

IT'S YOUR SPIDER, GARMADON, TELL IT TO BACK OFF!
UM, I CAN'T.
THEN I WILL!
LISTEN, LEGS, IT'S BEEN A LONG DAY...
KA-BAMM
AND I'VE HAD ENOUGH...
SO TAKE A BATH!
SPLOOSH
IF ONLY I COULD SOLVE ALL MY PROBLEMS THAT EASILY...

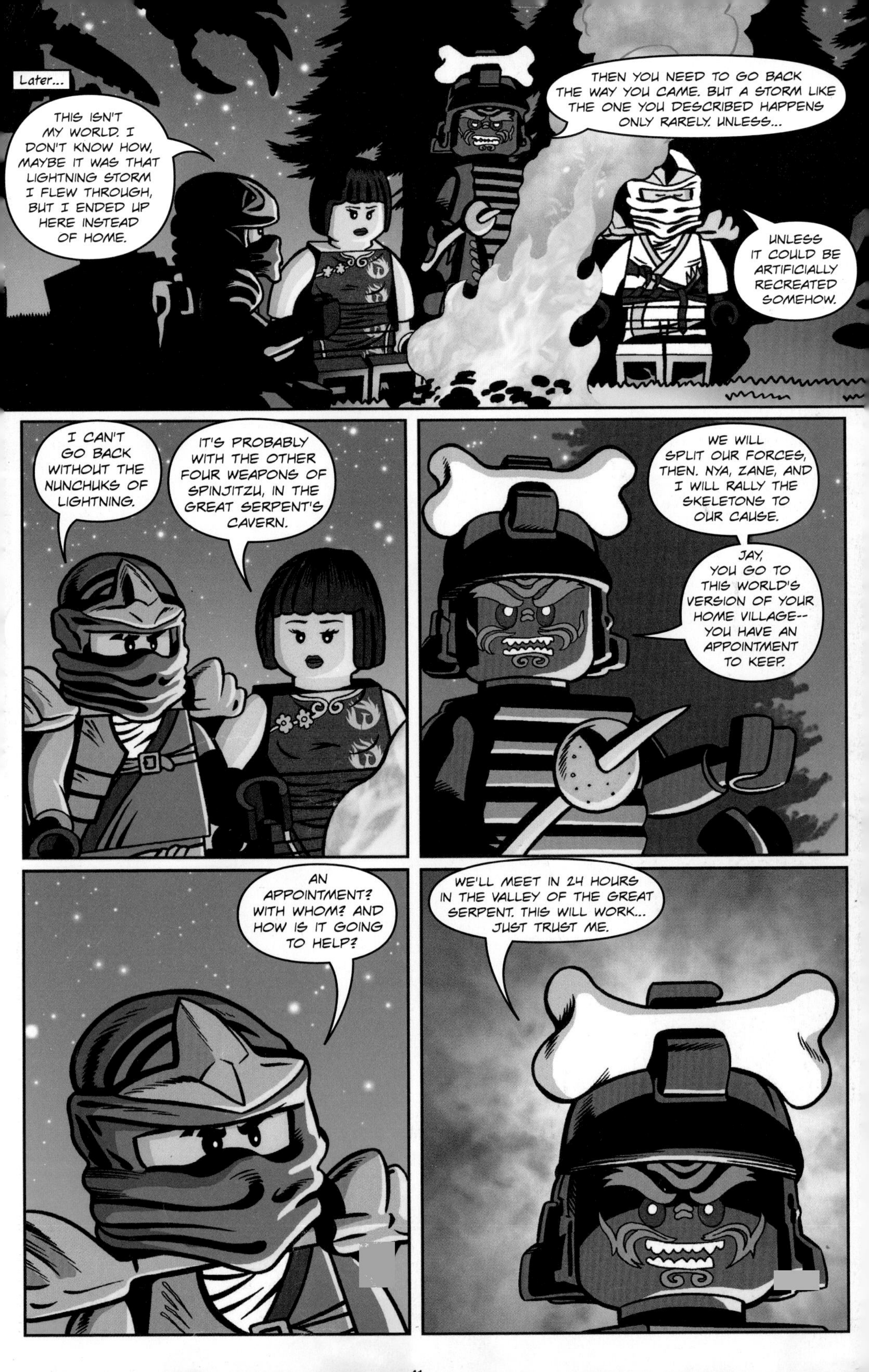
Later...
THIS ISN'T MY WORLD. I DON'T KNOW HOW, MAYBE IT WAS THAT LIGHTNING STORM I FLEW THROUGH, BUT I ENDED UP HERE INSTEAD OF HOME.
THEN YOU NEED TO GO BACK THE WAY YOU CAME. BUT A STORM LIKE THE ONE YOU DESCRIBED HAPPENS ONLY RARELY. UNLESS...
UNLESS IT COULD BE ARTIFICIALLY RECREATED SOMEHOW.
I CAN'T GO BACK WITHOUT THE NUNCHUKS OF LIGHTNING.
IT'S PROBABLY WITH THE OTHER FOUR WEAPONS OF SPINJITZU, IN THE GREAT SERPENT'S CAVERN.
WE WILL SPLIT OUR FORCES, THEN. NYA, ZANE, AND I WILL RALLY THE SKELETONS TO OUR CAUSE.
JAY, YOU GO TO THIS WORLD'S VERSION OF YOUR HOME VILLAGE-- YOU HAVE AN APPOINTMENT TO KEEP.
AN APPOINTMENT? WITH WHOM? AND HOW IS IT GOING TO HELP?
WE'LL MEET IN 24 HOURS IN THE VALLEY OF THE GREAT SERPENT. THIS WILL WORK... JUST TRUST ME.

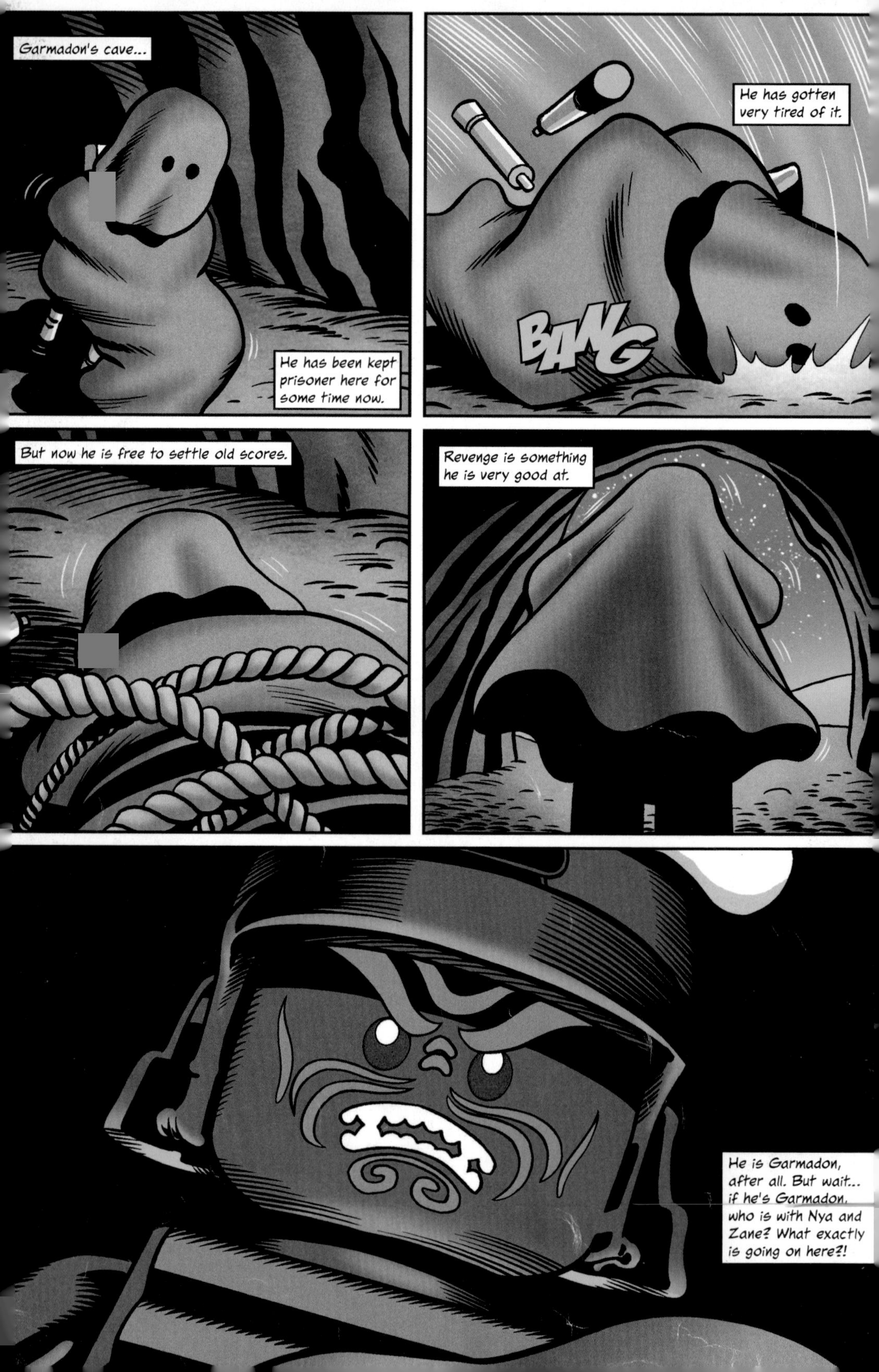

Garmadon's cave...
He has been kept prisoner here for some time now.
He has gotten very tired of it.
BANG
But now he is free to settle old scores.
Revenge is something he is very good at.
He is Garmadon, after all. But wait... if he's Garmadon, who is with Nya and Zane? What exactly is going on here?!

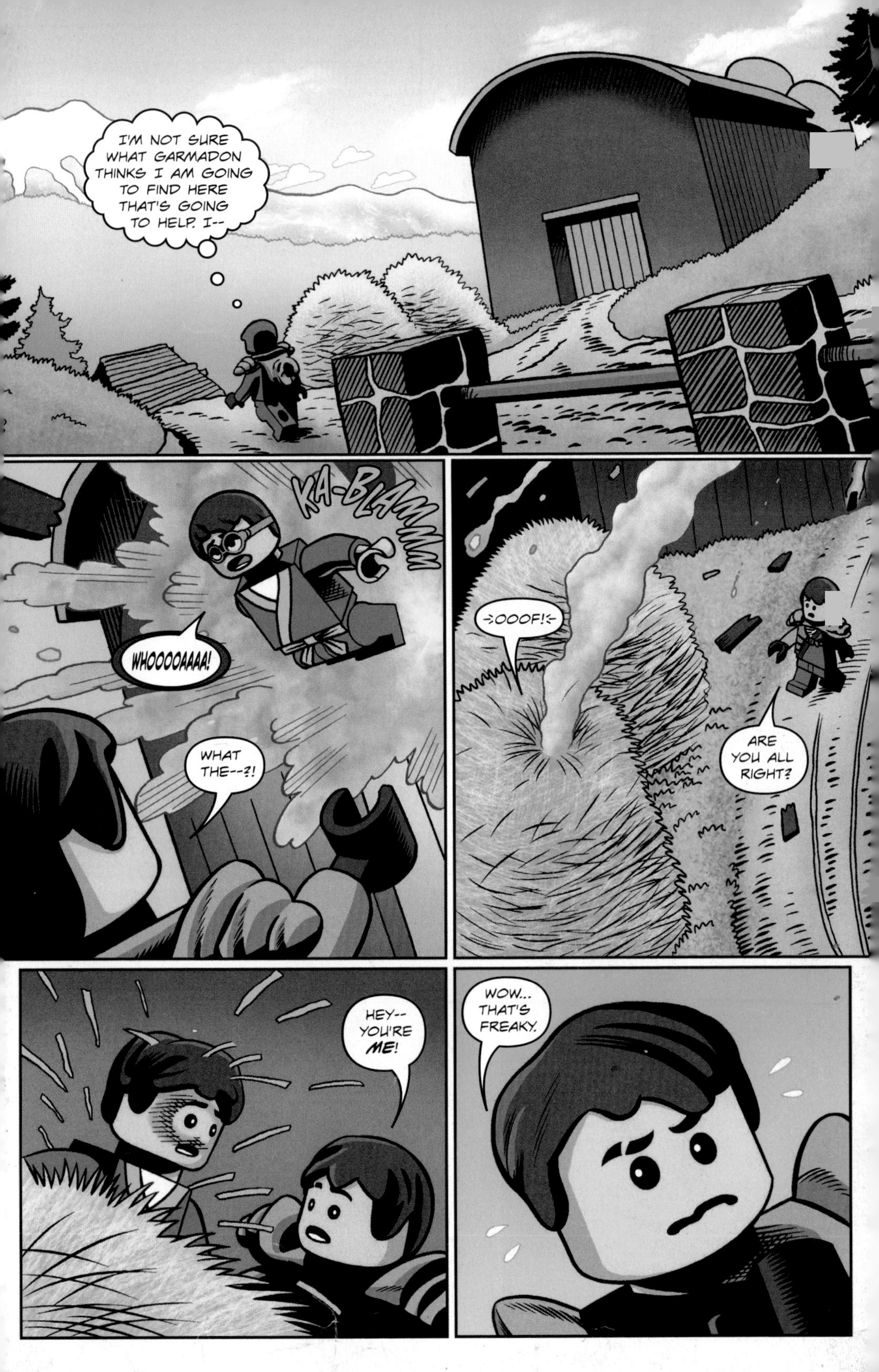
I'M NOT SURE WHAT GARMADON THINKS I AM GOING TO FIND HERE THAT'S GOING TO HELP. I--
KA-BLAMMM
WHOOOOAAAA!
WHAT THE--?!
OOOF!
ARE YOU ALL RIGHT?
HEY-- YOU'RE ME!
WOW... THAT'S FREAKY.

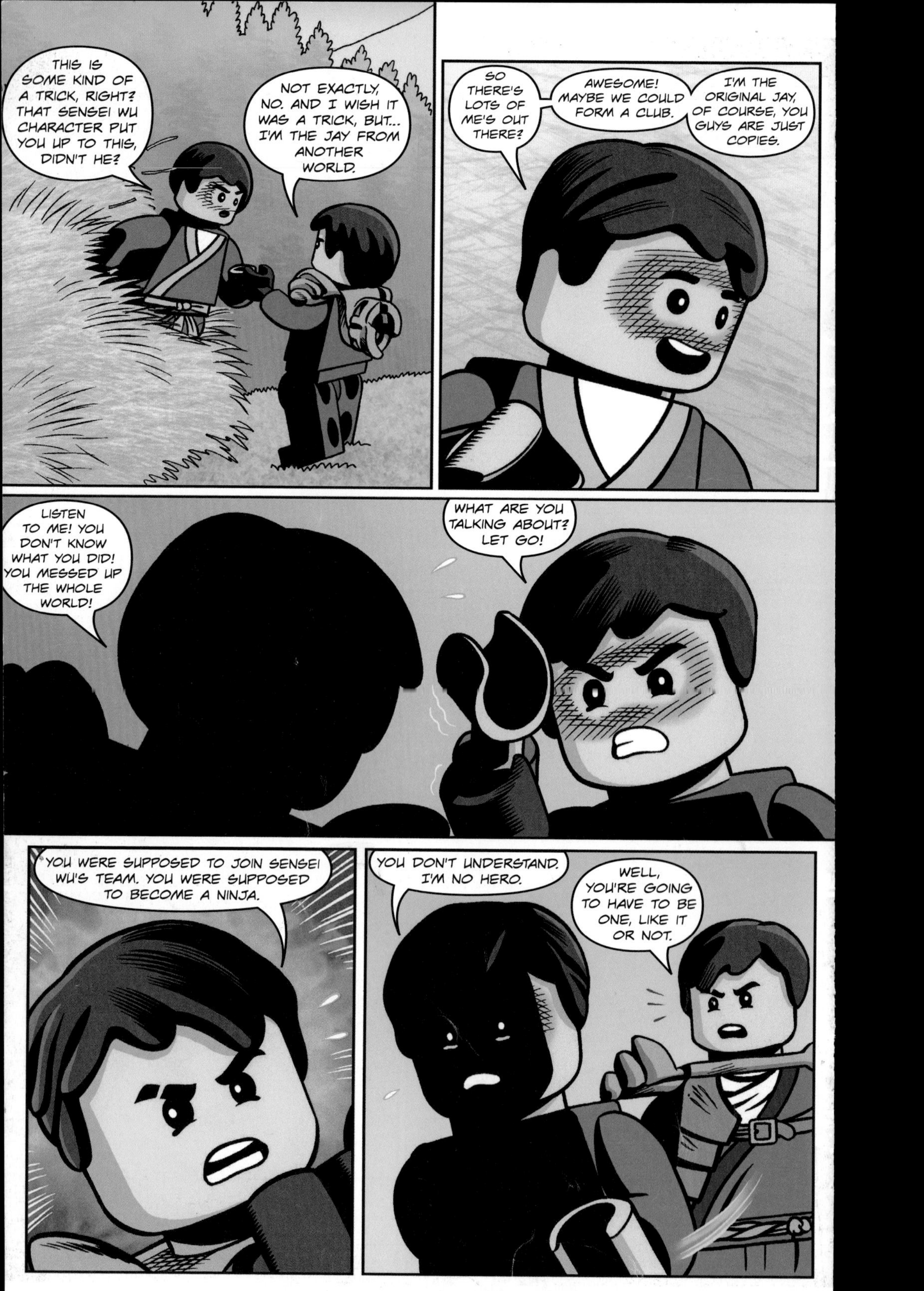
THIS IS SOME KIND OF A TRICK, RIGHT? THAT SENSEI WU CHARACTER PUT YOU UP TO THIS, DIDN'T HE?
NOT EXACTLY, NO. AND I WISH IT WAS A TRICK, BUT... I'M THE JAY FROM ANOTHER WORLD.
SO THERE'S LOTS OF ME'S OUT THERE?
AWESOME! MAYBE WE COULD FORM A CLUB.
I'M THE ORIGINAL JAY, OF COURSE, YOU GUYS ARE JUST COPIES.
LISTEN TO ME! YOU DON'T KNOW WHAT YOU DID! YOU MESSED UP THE WHOLE WORLD!
WHAT ARE YOU TALKING ABOUT? LET GO!
YOU WERE SUPPOSED TO JOIN SENSEI WU'S TEAM. YOU WERE SUPPOSED TO BECOME A NINJA.
YOU DON'T UNDERSTAND. I'M NO HERO.
WELL, YOU'RE GOING TO HAVE TO BE ONE, LIKE IT OR NOT.

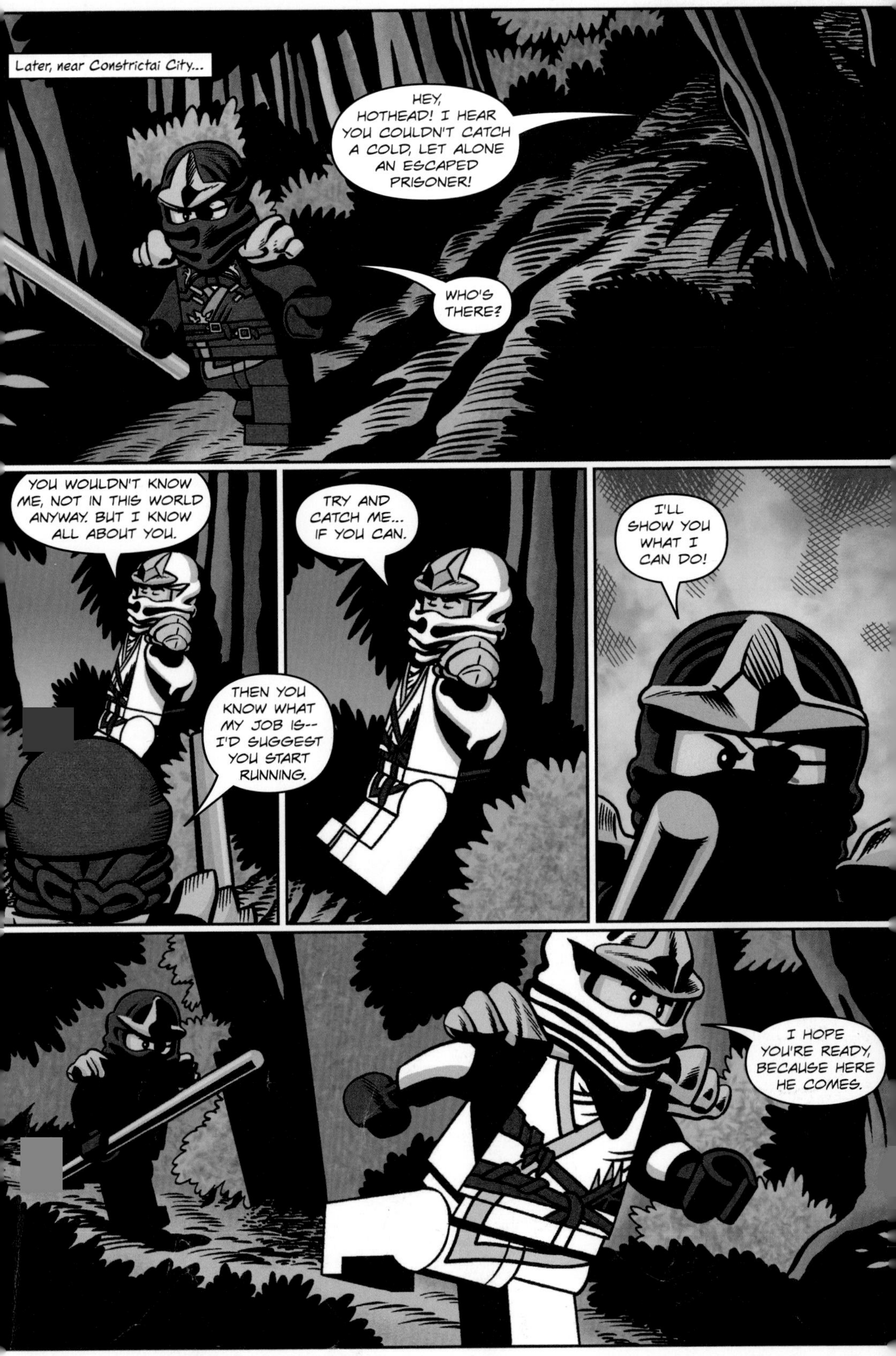

Later, near Constrictai City...
HEY, HOTHEAD! I HEAR YOU COULDN'T CATCH A COLD, LET ALONE AN ESCAPED PRISONER!
WHO'S THERE?
YOU WOULDN'T KNOW ME, NOT IN THIS WORLD ANYWAY. BUT I KNOW ALL ABOUT YOU.
THEN YOU KNOW WHAT MY JOB IS-- I'D SUGGEST YOU START RUNNING.
TRY AND CATCH ME... IF YOU CAN.
I'LL SHOW YOU WHAT I CAN DO!
I HOPE YOU'RE READY, BECAUSE HERE HE COMES.

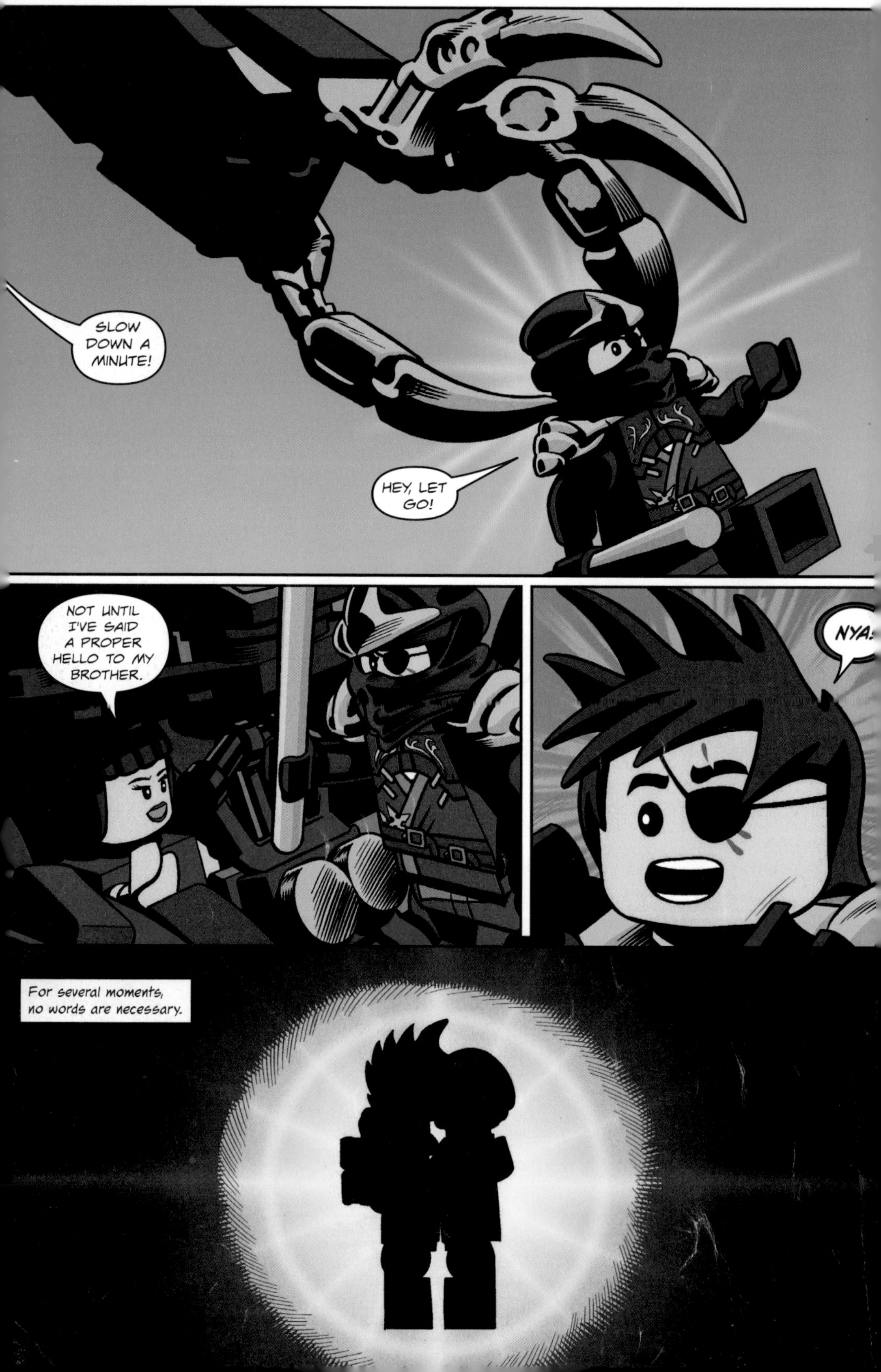
SLOW DOWN A MINUTE!
HEY, LET GO!
NOT UNTIL I'VE SAID A PROPER HELLO TO MY BROTHER.
NYA!
For several moments, no words are necessary.

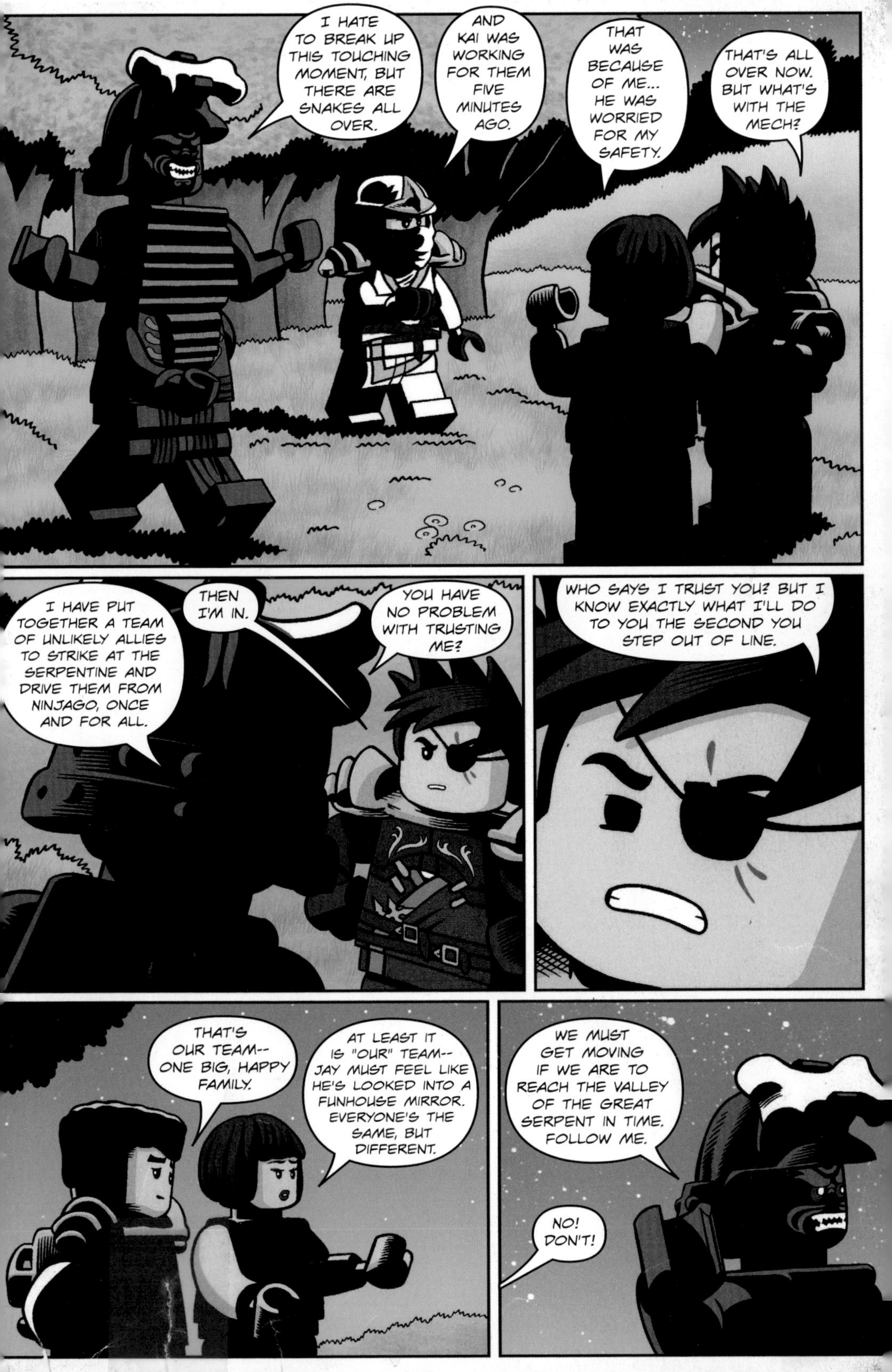
I HATE TO BREAK UP THIS TOUCHING MOMENT, BUT THERE ARE SNAKES ALL OVER.
AND KAI WAS WORKING FOR THEM FIVE MINUTES AGO.
THAT WAS BECAUSE OF ME... HE WAS WORRIED FOR MY SAFETY.
THAT'S ALL OVER NOW. BUT WHAT'S WITH THE MECH?
I HAVE PUT TOGETHER A TEAM OF UNLIKELY ALLIES TO STRIKE AT THE SERPENTINE AND DRIVE THEM FROM NINJAGO, ONCE AND FOR ALL.
THEN I'M IN.
YOU HAVE NO PROBLEM WITH TRUSTING ME?
WHO SAYS I TRUST YOU? BUT I KNOW EXACTLY WHAT I'LL DO TO YOU THE SECOND YOU STEP OUT OF LINE.
THAT'S OUR TEAM-- ONE BIG, HAPPY FAMILY.
AT LEAST IT IS "OUR" TEAM-- JAY MUST FEEL LIKE HE'S LOOKED INTO A FUNHOUSE MIRROR. EVERYONE'S THE SAME, BUT DIFFERENT.
WE MUST GET MOVING IF WE ARE TO REACH THE VALLEY OF THE GREAT SERPENT IN TIME. FOLLOW ME.
NO! DON'T!

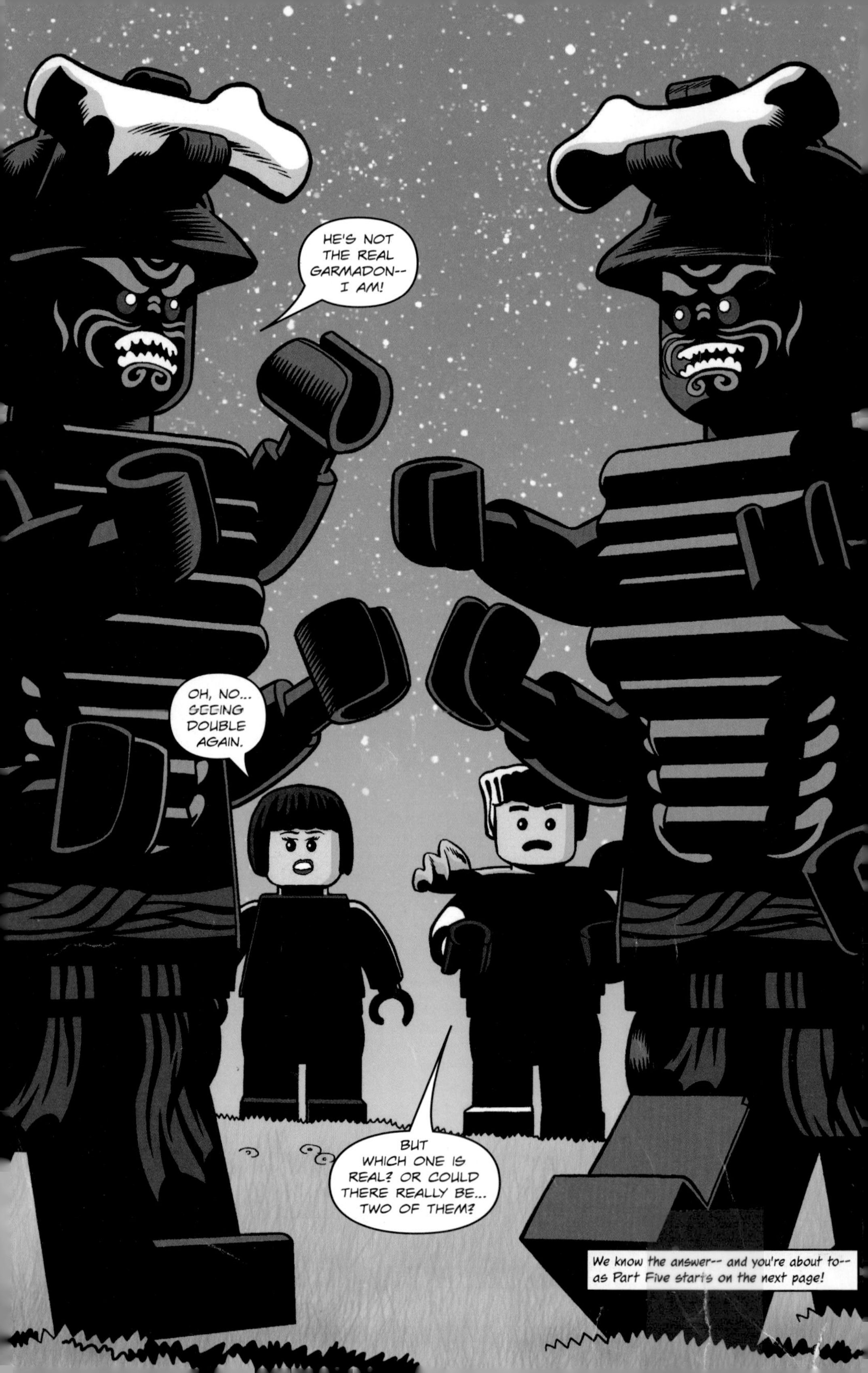
HE'S NOT THE REAL GARMADON-- I AM!
OH, NO... SEEING DOUBLE AGAIN.
BUT WHICH ONE IS REAL? OR COULD THERE REALLY BE... TWO OF THEM?
We know the answer-- and you're about to-- as Part Five starts on the next page!

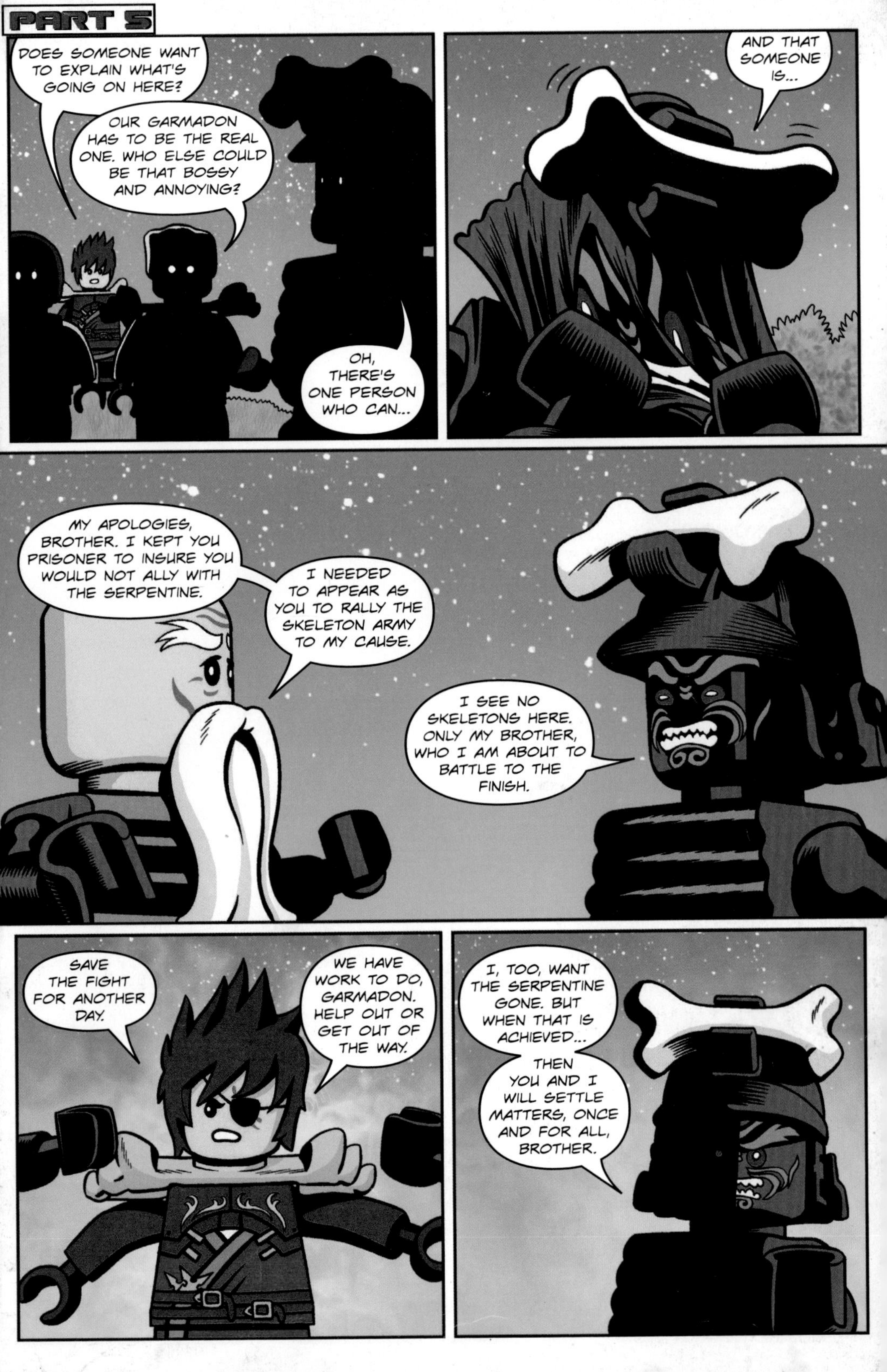
PART 5
DOES SOMEONE WANT TO EXPLAIN WHAT'S GOING ON HERE?
OUR GARMADON HAS TO BE THE REAL ONE. WHO ELSE COULD BE THAT BOSSY AND ANNOYING?
OH, THERE'S ONE PERSON WHO CAN...
AND THAT SOMEONE IS...
MY APOLOGIES, BROTHER. I KEPT YOU PRISONER TO INSURE YOU WOULD NOT ALLY WITH THE SERPENTINE.
I NEEDED TO APPEAR AS YOU TO RALLY THE SKELETON ARMY TO MY CAUSE.
I SEE NO SKELETONS HERE. ONLY MY BROTHER, WHO I AM ABOUT TO BATTLE TO THE FINISH.
SAVE THE FIGHT FOR ANOTHER DAY.
WE HAVE WORK TO DO, GARMADON. HELP OUT OR GET OUT OF THE WAY.
I, TOO, WANT THE SERPENTINE GONE. BUT WHEN THAT IS ACHIEVED...
THEN YOU AND I WILL SETTLE MATTERS, ONCE AND FOR ALL, BROTHER.

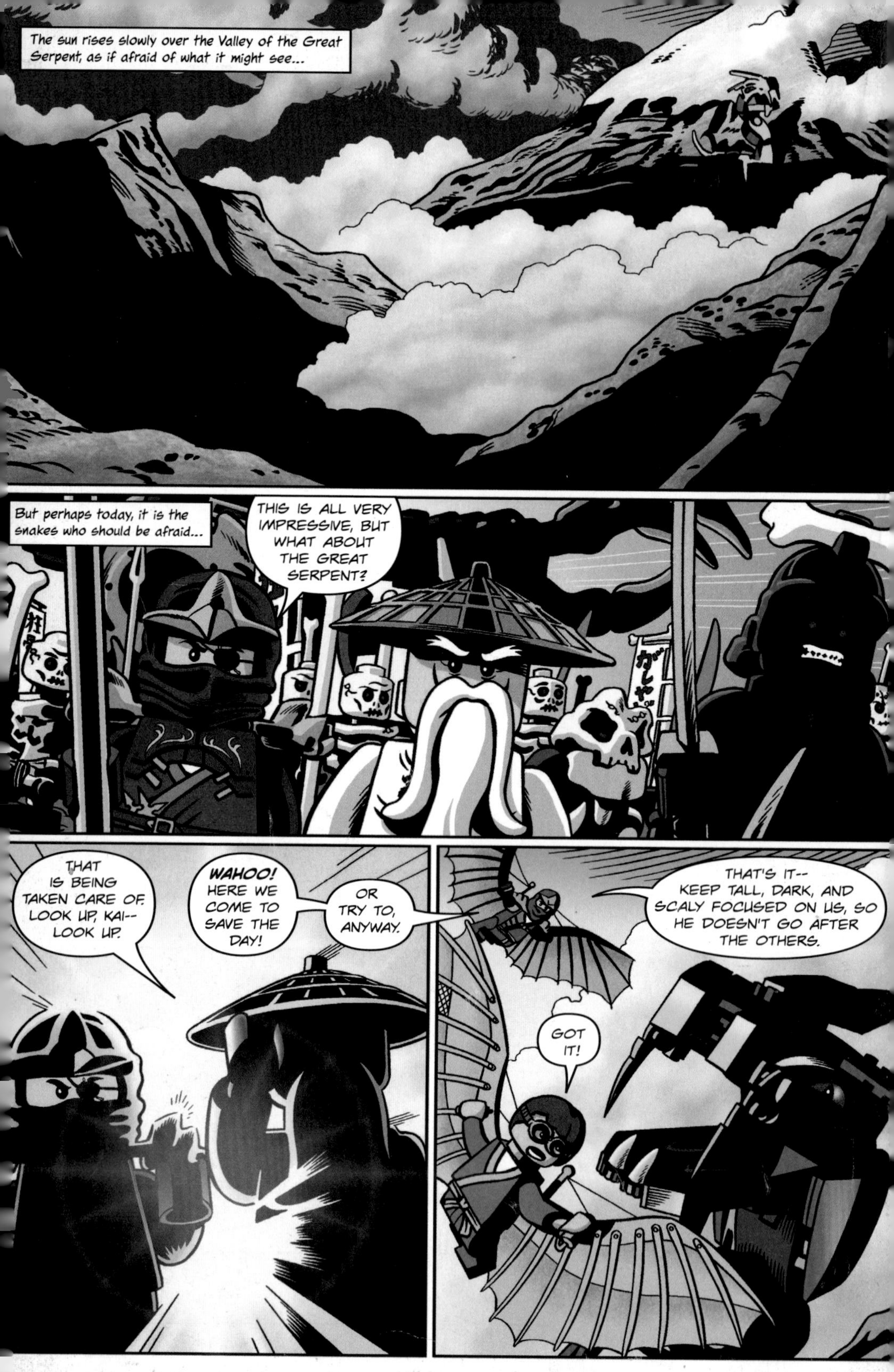
The sun rises slowly over the Valley of the Great Serpent, as if afraid of what it might see...
But perhaps today, it is the snakes who should be afraid...
THIS IS ALL VERY IMPRESSIVE, BUT WHAT ABOUT THE GREAT SERPENT?
THAT IS BEING TAKEN CARE OF. LOOK UP, KAI-- LOOK UP.
WAHOO! HERE WE COME TO SAVE THE DAY!
OR TRY TO, ANYWAY.
THAT'S IT-- KEEP TALL, DARK, AND SCALY FOCUSED ON US, SO HE DOESN'T GO AFTER THE OTHERS.
GOT IT!

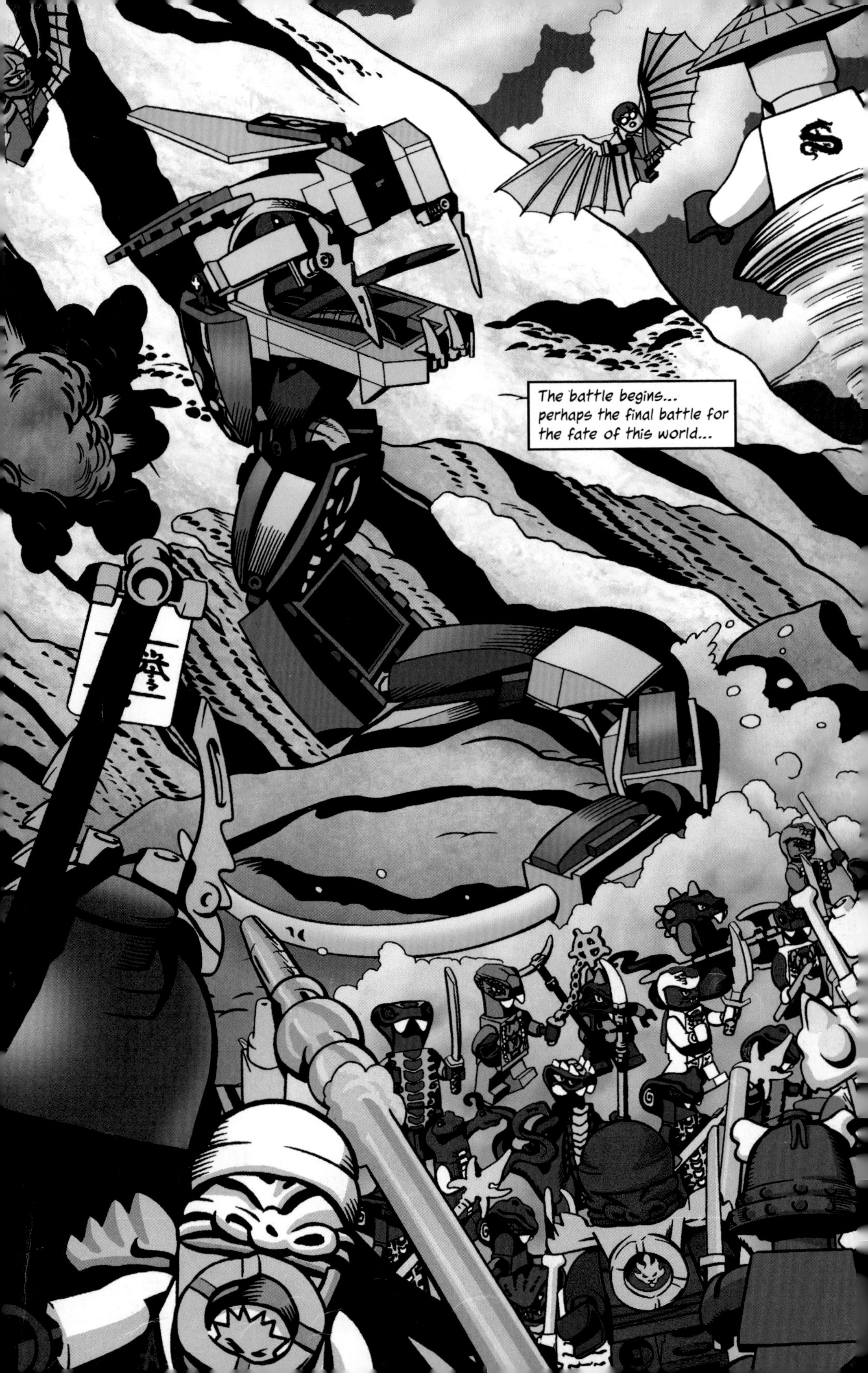
The battle begins... perhaps the final battle for the fate of this world...

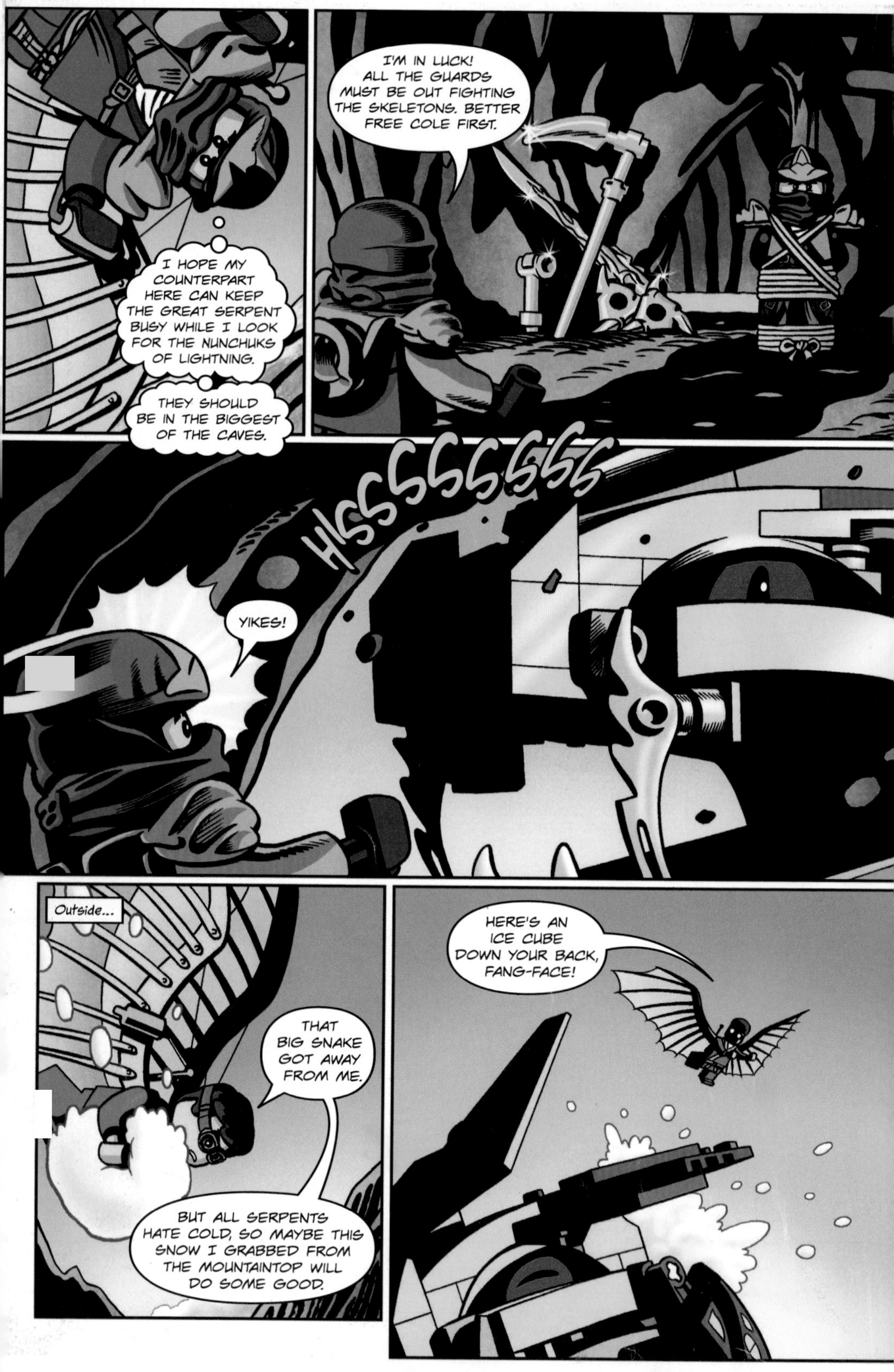
I HOPE MY COUNTERPART HERE CAN KEEP THE GREAT SERPENT BUSY WHILE I LOOK FOR THE NUNCHUKS OF LIGHTNING.
THEY SHOULD BE IN THE BIGGEST OF THE CAVES.
I'M IN LUCK! ALL THE GUARDS MUST BE OUT FIGHTING THE SKELETONS. BETTER FREE COLE FIRST.
HISSSSSSSS
YIKES!
Outside...
THAT BIG SNAKE GOT AWAY FROM ME.
BUT ALL SERPENTS HATE COLD, SO MAYBE THIS SNOW I GRABBED FROM THE MOUNTAINTOP WILL DO SOME GOOD.
HERE'S AN ICE CUBE DOWN YOUR BACK, FANG-FACE!

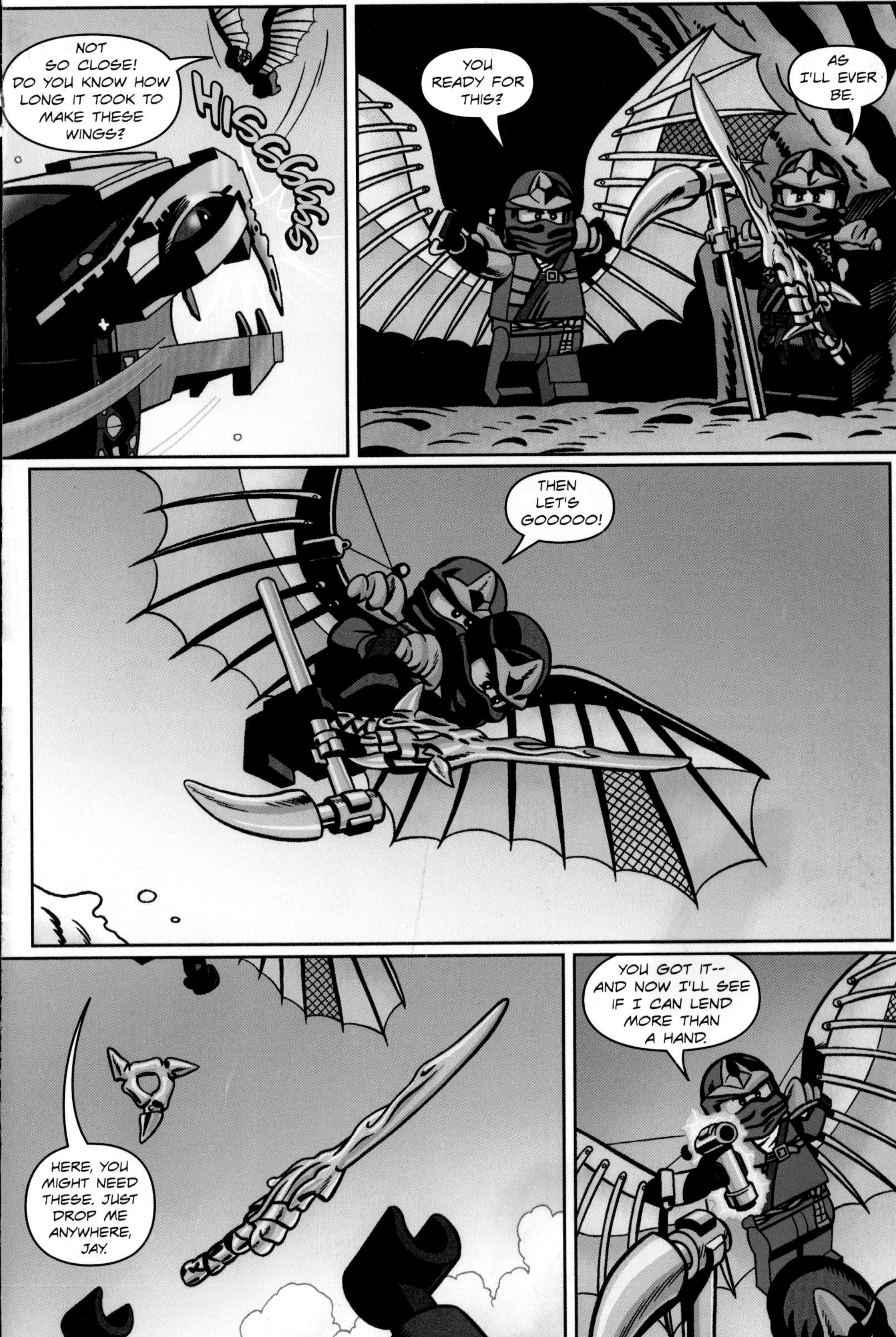
NOT SO CLOSE! DO YOU KNOW HOW LONG IT TOOK TO MAKE THESE WINGS?
HISSSSSS
YOU READY FOR THIS?
AS I'LL EVER BE.
THEN LET'S GOOOOO!
HERE, YOU MIGHT NEED THESE. JUST DROP ME ANYWHERE, JAY.
YOU GOT IT-- AND NOW I'LL SEE IF I CAN LEND MORE THAN A HAND.

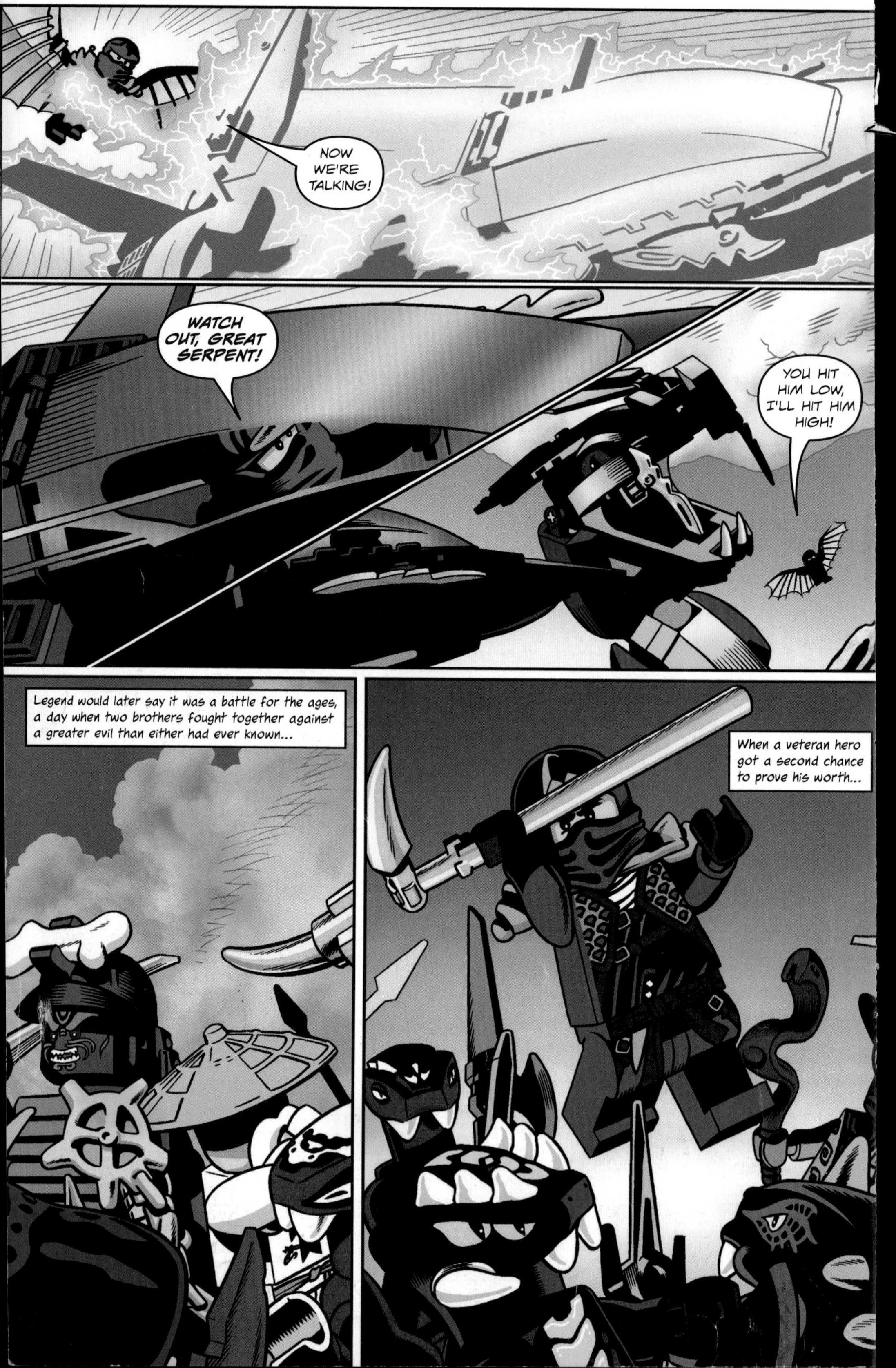
NOW WE'RE TALKING!
WATCH OUT, GREAT SERPENT!
YOU HIT HIM LOW, I'LL HIT HIM HIGH!
Legend would later say it was a battle for the ages, a day when two brothers fought together against a greater evil than either had ever known...
When a veteran hero got a second chance to prove his worth...

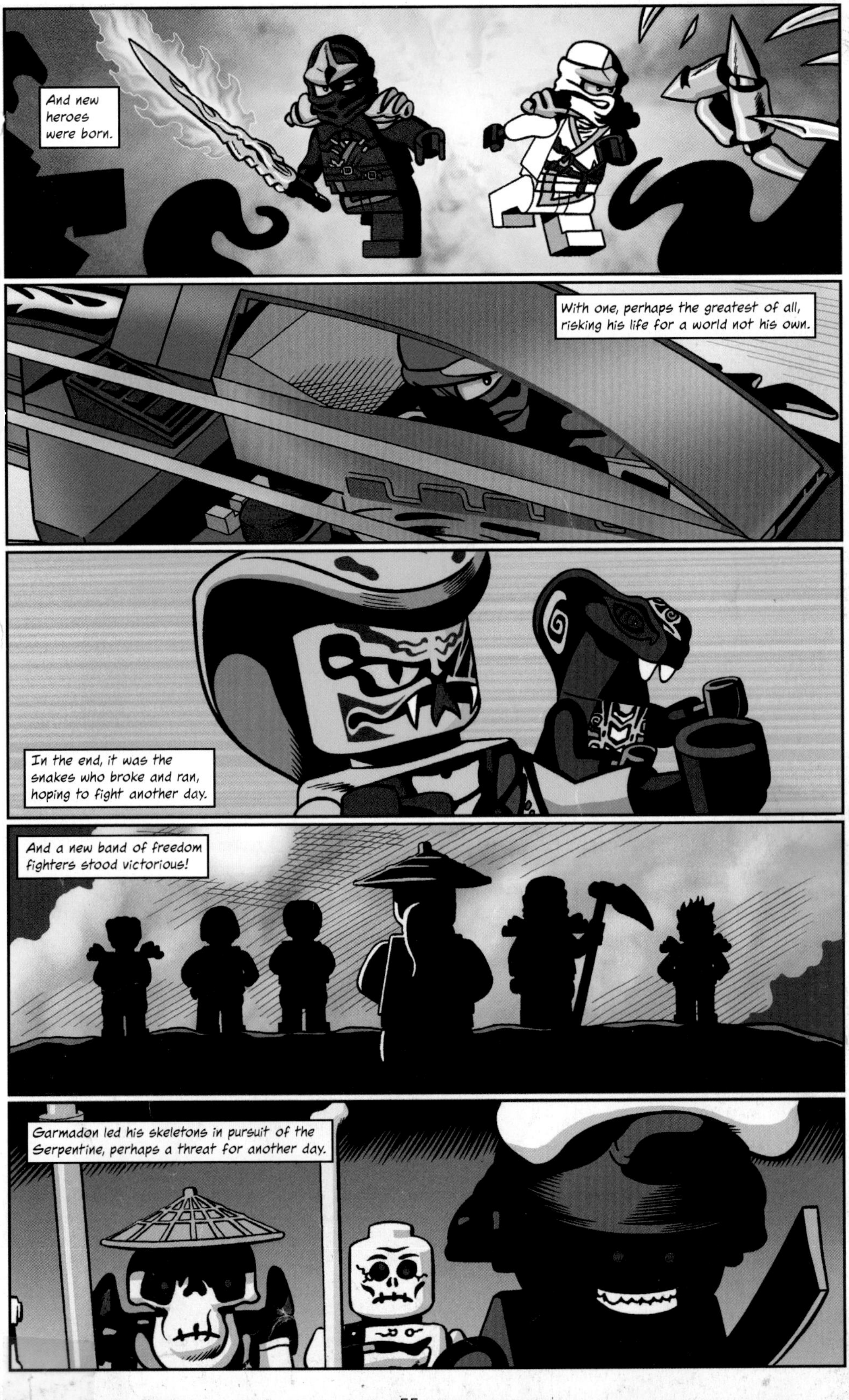
And new heroes were born.
With one, perhaps the greatest of all, risking his life for a world not his own.
In the end, it was the snakes who broke and ran, hoping to fight another day.
And a new band of freedom fighters stood victorious!
Garmadon led his skeletons in pursuit of the Serpentine, perhaps a threat for another day.

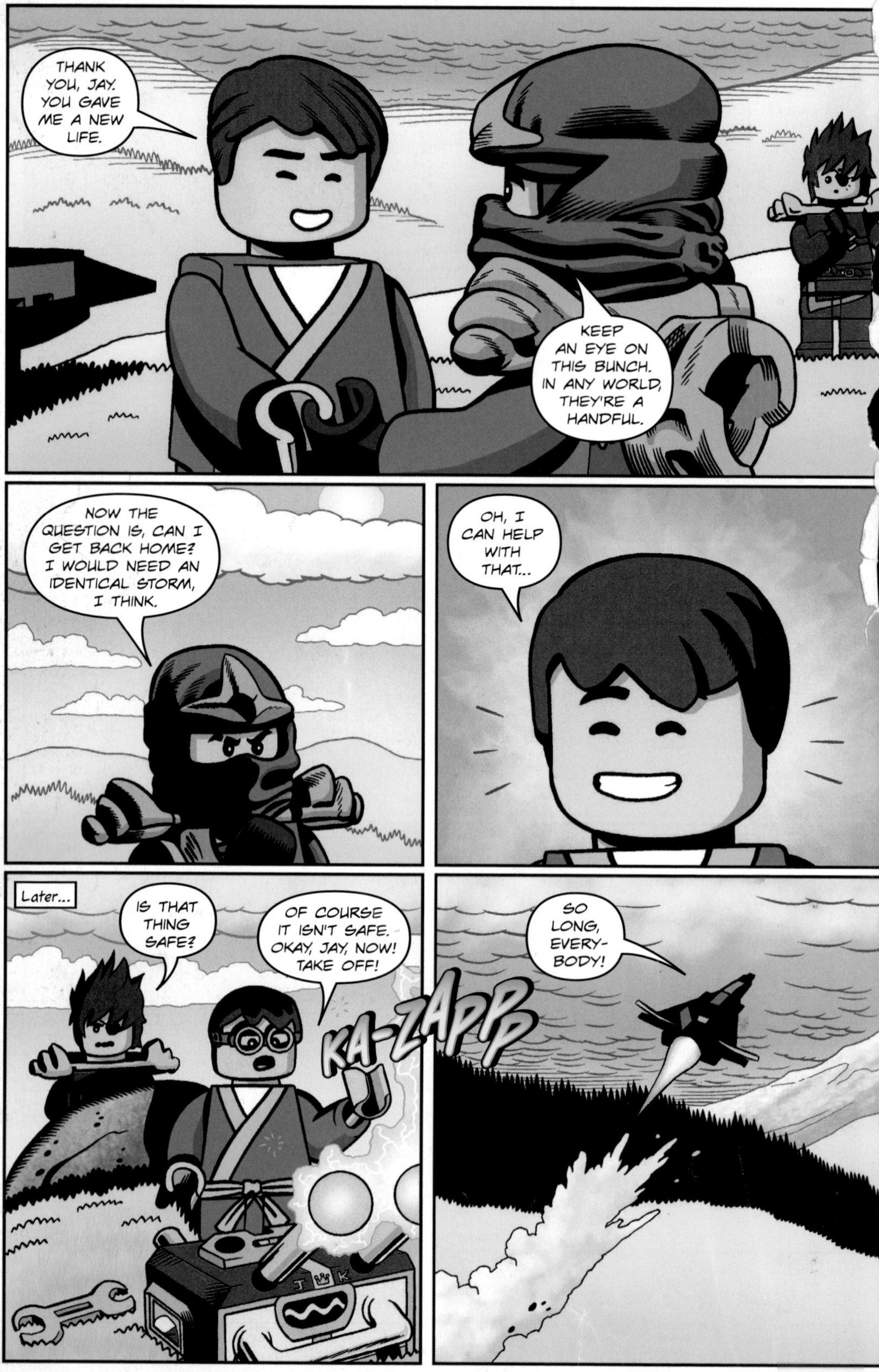
THANK YOU, JAY. YOU GAVE ME A NEW LIFE.
KEEP AN EYE ON THIS BUNCH. IN ANY WORLD, THEY'RE A HANDFUL.
NOW THE QUESTION IS, CAN I GET BACK HOME? I WOULD NEED AN IDENTICAL STORM, I THINK.
OH, I CAN HELP WITH THAT...
Later...
IS THAT THING SAFE?
OF COURSE IT ISN'T SAFE. OKAY, JAY, NOW! TAKE OFF!
KA-ZAPPP
SO LONG, EVERY-BODY!

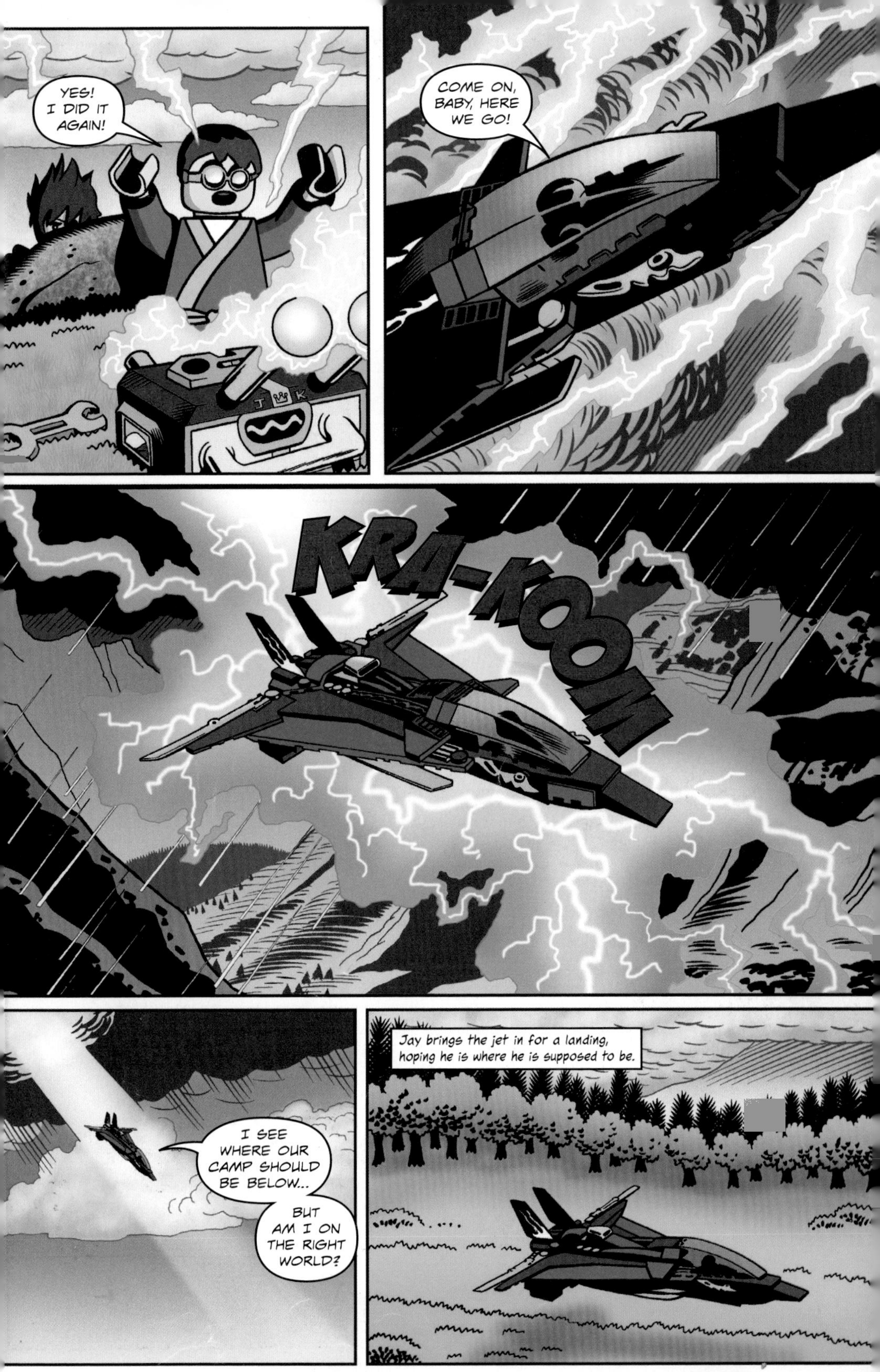
YES! I DID IT AGAIN!
COME ON, BABY, HERE WE GO!
KRA-KOOM
I SEE WHERE OUR CAMP SHOULD BE BELOW...
BUT AM I ON THE RIGHT WORLD?
Jay brings the jet in for a landing, hoping he is where he is supposed to be.

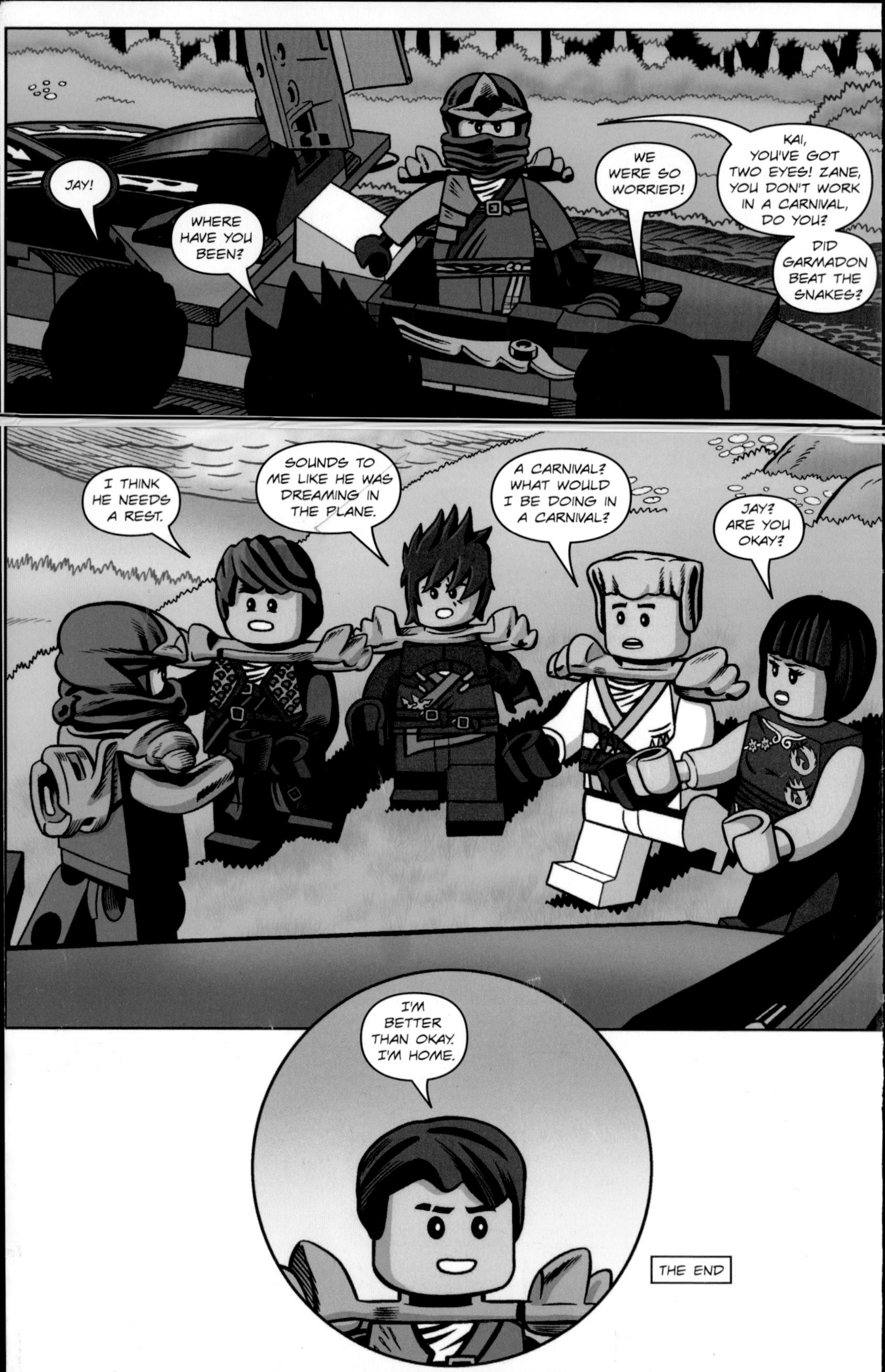
JAY!
WHERE HAVE YOU BEEN?
WE WERE SO WORRIED!
KAI, YOU'VE GOT TWO EYES! ZANE, YOU DON'T WORK IN A CARNIVAL, DO YOU?
DID GARMADON BEAT THE SNAKES?
I THINK HE NEEDS A REST.
SOUNDS TO ME LIKE HE WAS DREAMING IN THE PLANE.
A CARNIVAL? WHAT WOULD I BE DOING IN A CARNIVAL?
JAY? ARE YOU OKAY?
I'M BETTER THAN OKAY. I'M HOME.
THE END

WATCH OUT FOR PAPERCUTZ™

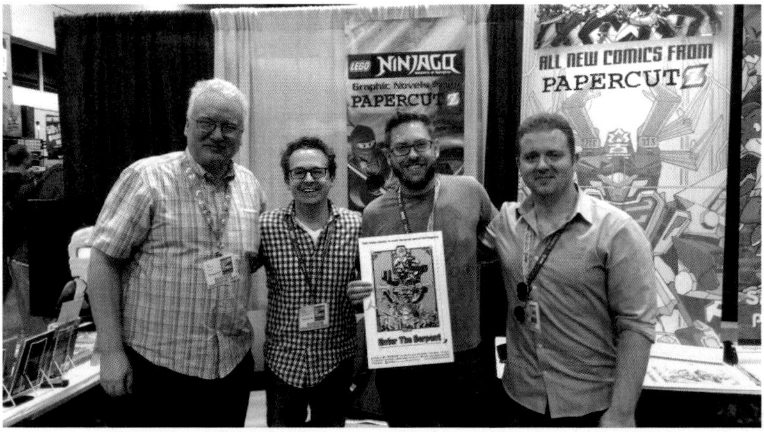

LEGO NINJAGO
PAPERCUTZ
ALL NEW COMICS FROM
PAPERCUTZ

Jim Salicrup, The Hageman Brothers, and Michael Petranek at the Papercutz Booth at the San Diego Comic-Con.

Welcome to the fifth, fabulous LEGO® NINJAGO graphic novel from Papercutz, the company dedicated to publishing great graphic novels for all ages. I'm Jim Salicrup, Papercutz Editor-in-Chief and snakeskin shoe-shiner. We've got lots of exciting NINJAGO-related things to talk about, so let's get right to it!

Every year since Papercutz started publishing back in 2005, we've also exhibited at the world-famous Comic-Con International: San Diego, or as it's more commonly called, the San Diego Comic-Con. Being one of the new kids on the block, we tend to get overshadowed by the older, bigger comicbook publishers and their expensive big booths, which in turn tend to get dwarfed by the really big booths brought in by various movie studios/comicbook publishers and major toy companies, toy companies such as The LEGO Group! But the show is all about the fans getting to see, and sometimes even meet, their favorite movie and TV stars, and comicbook writers and artists. And even cooler than that, getting cool free stuff available only at Comic-Con!

Well, this year, Papercutz had a couple of cool free Comic-Con exclusives, as they're called. One was an Ash-Can Edition of the upcoming NANCY DREW AND THE CLUE CREW graphic novel series, and the other was a special free LEGO NINJAGO poster, inspired by a classic martial arts movie poster, and drawn and colored by Jolyon Yates. Not only were LEGO NINJAGO fans thrilled with this surprise Papercutz premium, but even the writers of the hit LEGO Ninjago TV series, the Hageman Brothers, seemed happy with it (see photo). While we can't give each and everyone of you one of these posters, we can do the next best thing. Just go to page 64 and check out the poster everyone is talking about! It follows the special preview of LEGO NINJAGO #6 "Warriors of Stone."

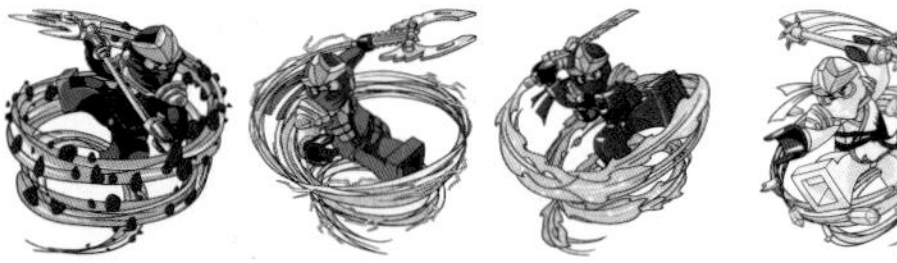

So, until next time, keep spinnin'!

Thanks,

Jim

STAY IN TOUCH!

EMAIL:	salicrup@papercutz.com
WEB:	www.papercutz.com
TWITTER:	@papercutzgn
FACEBOOK:	PAPERCUTZGRAPHICNOVELS
SNAIL MAIL:	Papercutz, 160 Broadway, Suite 700, East Wing, New York, NY 10038

Special Preview of LEGO® NINJAGO #6 "Warriors of Stone"...

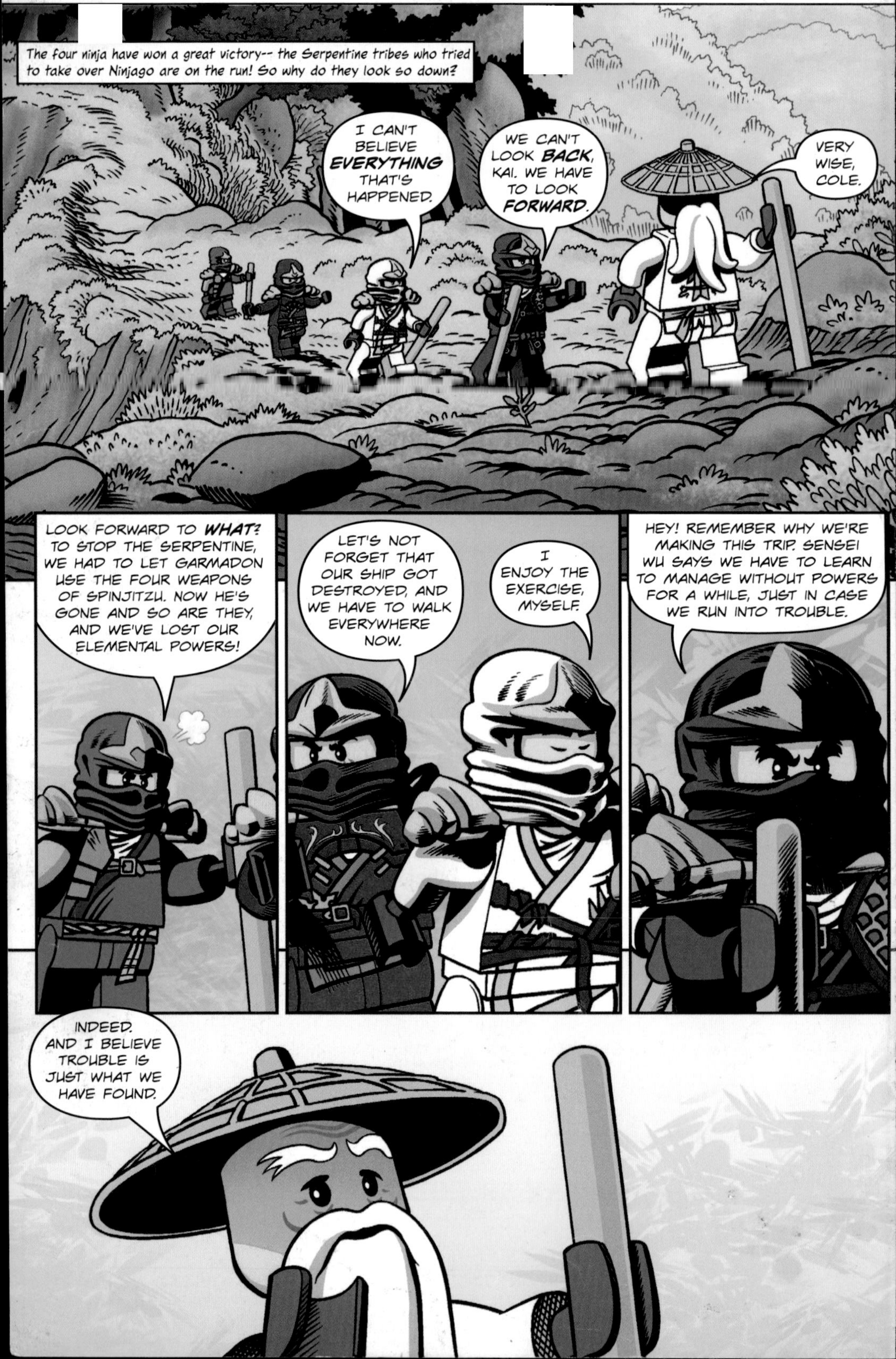
The four ninja have won a great victory-- the Serpentine tribes who tried to take over Ninjago are on the run! So why do they look so down?
I CAN'T BELIEVE EVERYTHING THAT'S HAPPENED.
WE CAN'T LOOK BACK, KAI. WE HAVE TO LOOK FORWARD.
VERY WISE, COLE.
LOOK FORWARD TO WHAT? TO STOP THE SERPENTINE, WE HAD TO LET GARMADON USE THE FOUR WEAPONS OF SPINJITZU. NOW HE'S GONE AND SO ARE THEY, AND WE'VE LOST OUR ELEMENTAL POWERS!
LET'S NOT FORGET THAT OUR SHIP GOT DESTROYED, AND WE HAVE TO WALK EVERYWHERE NOW.
I ENJOY THE EXERCISE, MYSELF.
HEY! REMEMBER WHY WE'RE MAKING THIS TRIP. SENSEI WU SAYS WE HAVE TO LEARN TO MANAGE WITHOUT POWERS FOR A WHILE, JUST IN CASE WE RUN INTO TROUBLE.
INDEED. AND I BELIEVE TROUBLE IS JUST WHAT WE HAVE FOUND.

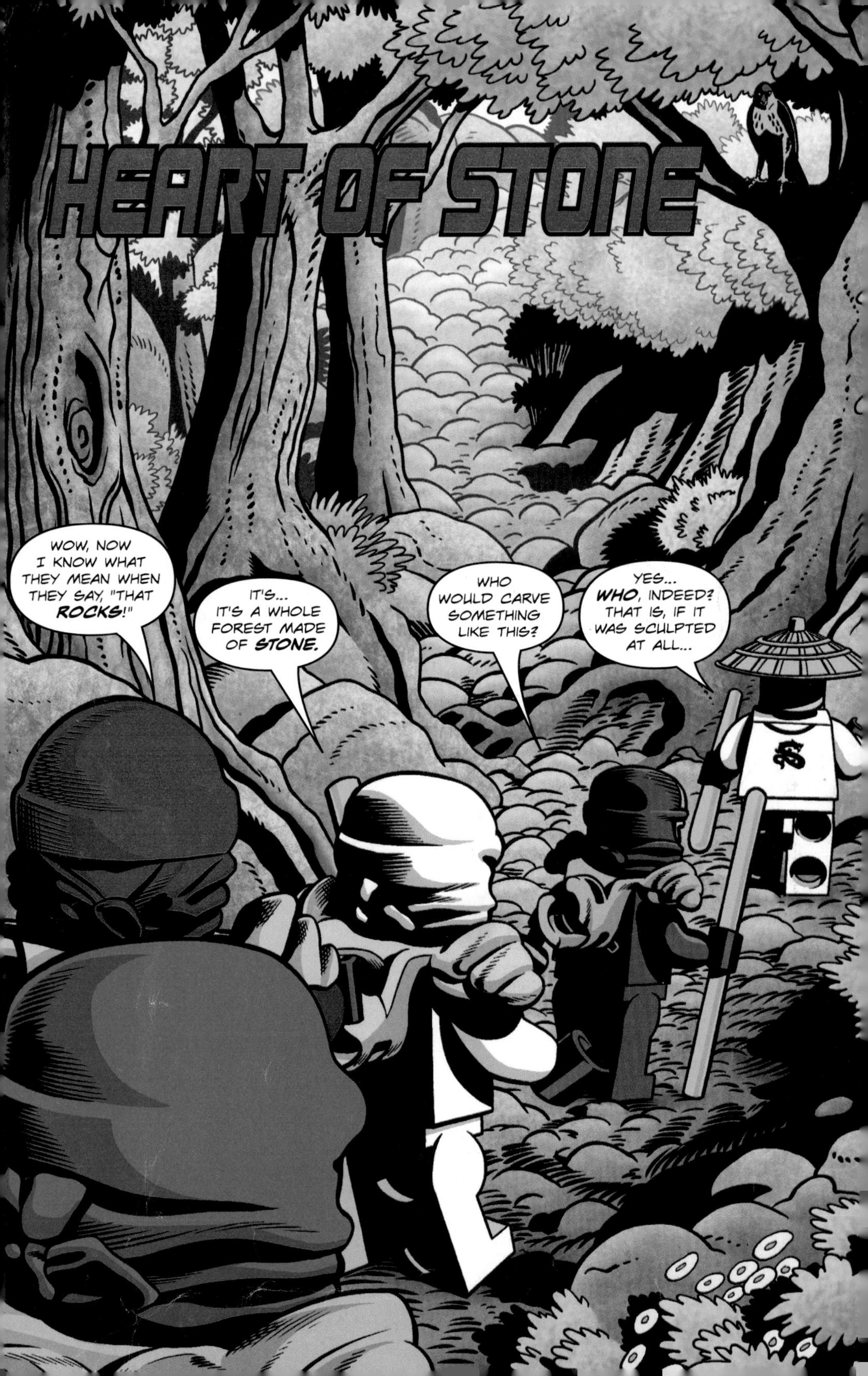
HEART OF STONE
WOW, NOW I KNOW WHAT THEY MEAN WHEN THEY SAY, "THAT ROCKS!"
IT'S... IT'S A WHOLE FOREST MADE OF STONE.
WHO WOULD CARVE SOMETHING LIKE THIS?
YES... WHO, INDEED? THAT IS, IF IT WAS SCULPTED AT ALL...

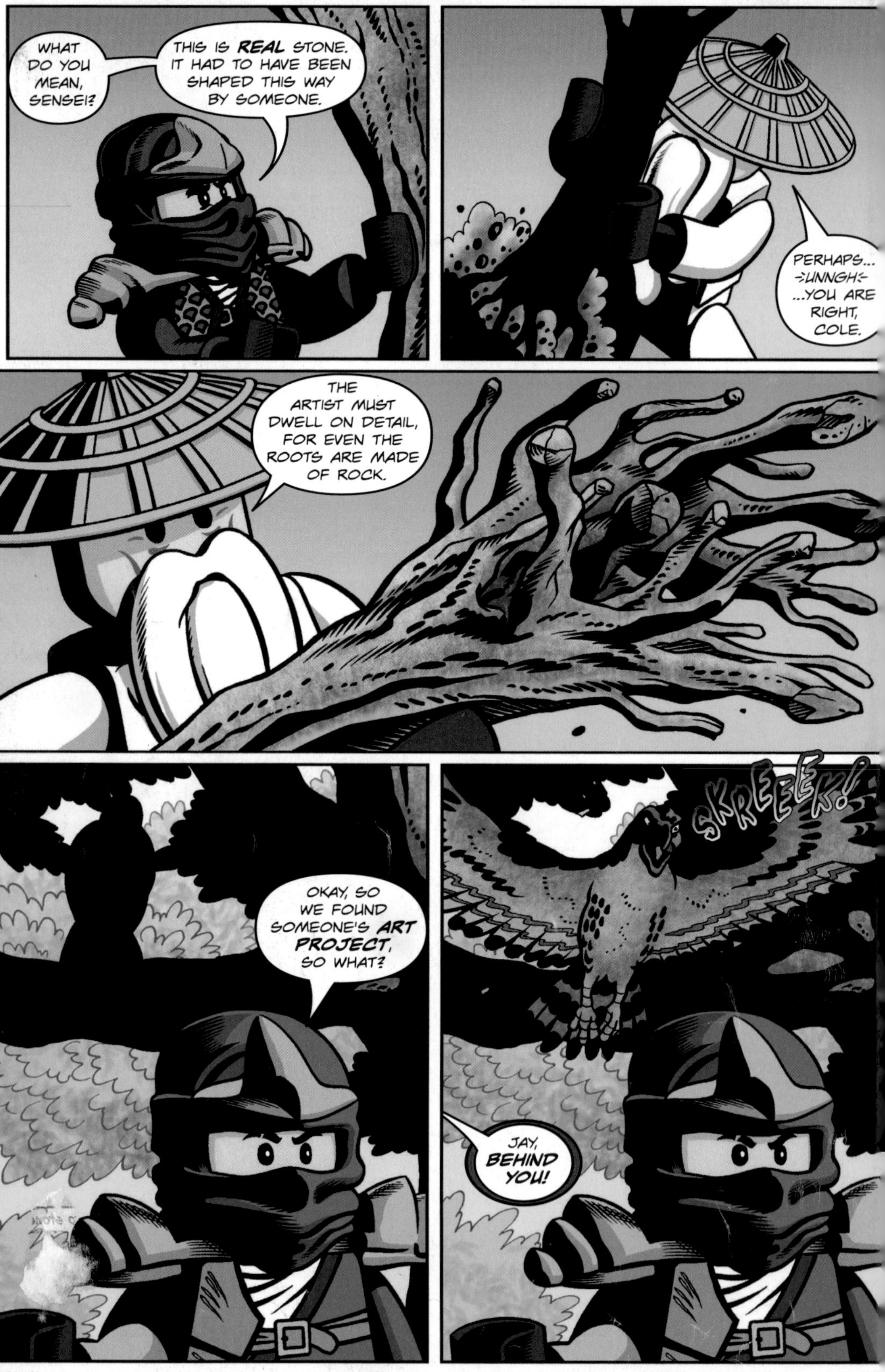
WHAT DO YOU MEAN, SENSEI?
THIS IS **REAL** STONE. IT HAD TO HAVE BEEN SHAPED THIS WAY BY SOMEONE.
PERHAPS... -UNNGH- ...YOU ARE RIGHT, COLE.
THE ARTIST MUST DWELL ON DETAIL, FOR EVEN THE ROOTS ARE MADE OF ROCK.
OKAY, SO WE FOUND SOMEONE'S **ART PROJECT**, SO WHAT?
SKREEEEK!
JAY, **BEHIND YOU!**

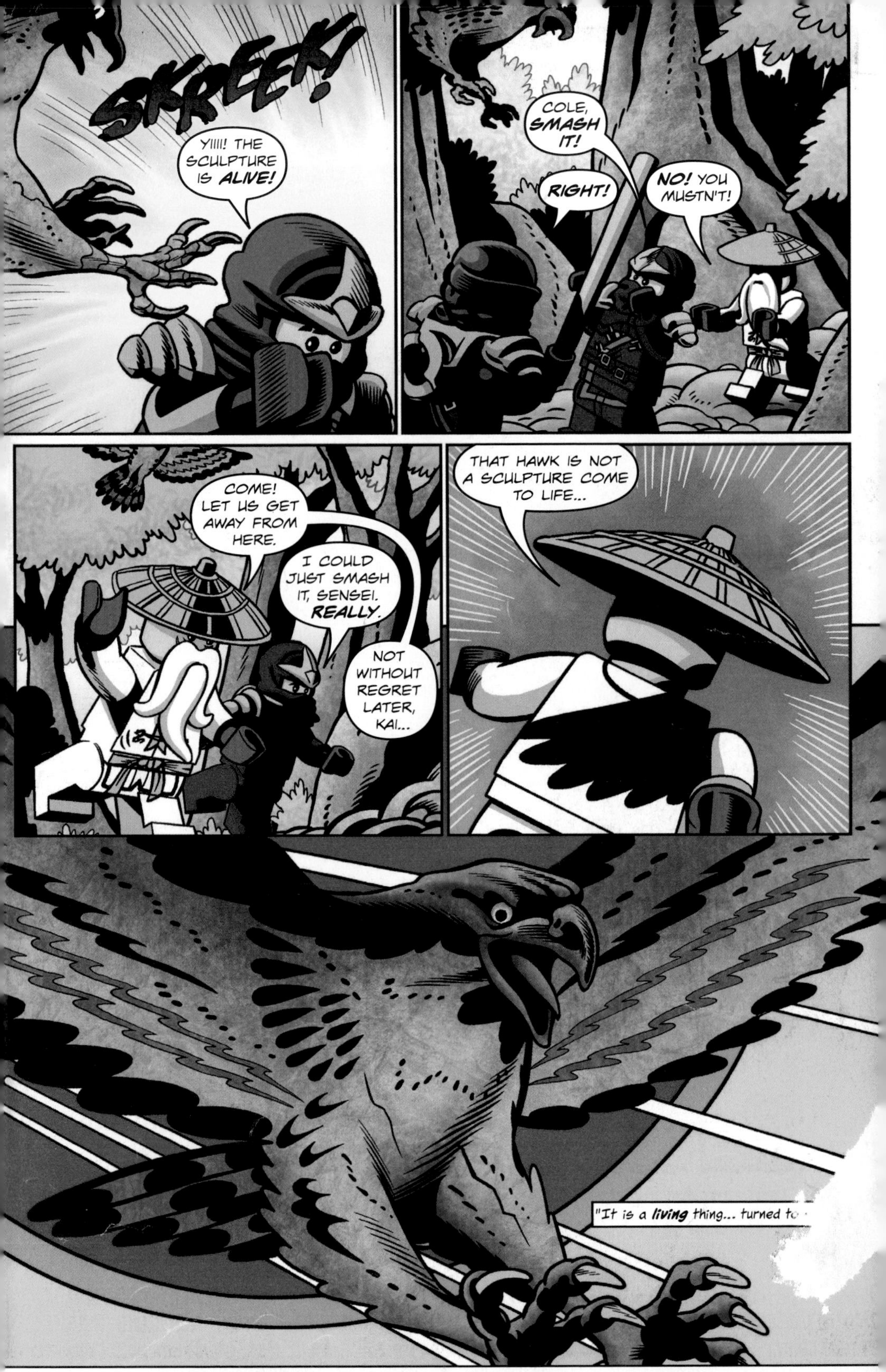
SKREEK!
YIIII! THE SCULPTURE IS *ALIVE!*
COLE, *SMASH IT!*
RIGHT!
NO! YOU MUSTN'T!
COME! LET US GET AWAY FROM HERE.
I COULD JUST SMASH IT, SENSEI. *REALLY*.
NOT WITHOUT REGRET LATER, KAI...
THAT HAWK IS NOT A SCULPTURE COME TO LIFE...
"It is a *living* thing... turned to

Don't Miss LEGO® NINJAGO #6 "Warriors of Stone"!

Their deadly mission: to crack the secret nest of the Fangpyre!

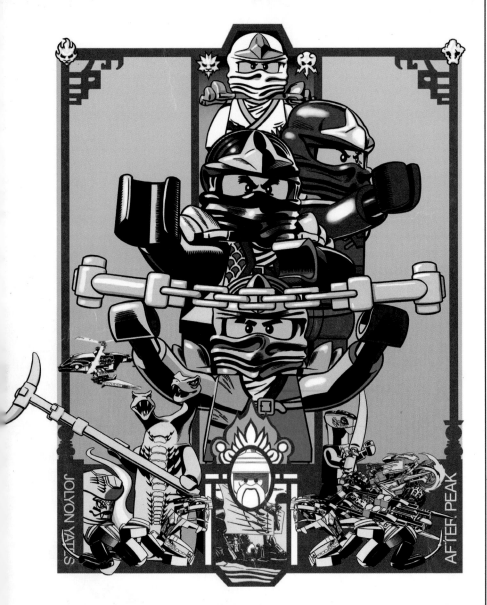

JOLYON YATES

AFTER PEAK

Enter The Serpent

The ultimate brick masterpiece! Lavishly produced on location in the world of LEGO® Ninjago!

KAI JAY COLE AND ZANE IN "ENTER THE SERPENT" CO-STARRING SENSEI WU AND INTRODUCING LLOYD GARMADON WRITTEN BY GREG FARSHTEY DIRECTED BY JOLYON YATES

VISUAL EFFECTS BY JAYJAY JACKSON DIALOGUE COACH BRYAN SENKA LINE PRODUCER MICHAEL PETRANEK WEAPONS CONSULTANT JESSE POST EDITED BY JIM SALICRUP EXECUTIVE PRODUCER HELLE REIMERS HOLM-JORGENSEN

PRODUCED BY TERRY NANTIER A LEGO NINJAGO PRODUCTION IN ASSOCIATION WITH PAPERCUTZ